SEVEN
SHORT STORIES

: : :

GORDON WILLIAMS

SEVEN SHORT STORIES

Published 2023 by Gordon Williams
Copyright © Gordon Williams 2023
All rights reserved

Print ISBN 978-1-8383039-4-5
eBook ISBN 978-1-8383039-5-2

www.gordonwilliams.uk

: : :

Set in 10.5pt Source Serif Pro
Titles set in Cinzel

CONTENTS

Room 33 was his room now. It had been empty for two days, since Bill Warwick had moved on. On day one Frank sat at the desk and looked out of the wide window over the square; it was grim – the view, the job, the pay. But it was a prison after all, and it was work, and he'd needed work. The desk was bare when he'd walked in, not even an in-tray, or a phone, and mostly empty drawers until Matilda came with a box – pens, stapler, office stuff. But no phone. "I'm next door," she'd said. "If you need anything, ask me."

She was a thirty-something Prison Office Manager who obviously got on with things, and who explained to him what was required, and what was not. He was told to call her Ma'am, like royalty. And Frank already wondered how long he could stick it, being just out of University and wishing someone somewhere would need a Film Studies graduate, but he'd had to find something, and this was it. Then she came back and dropped a heavy book onto his desk, and showed him a pile of papers.

"These are requests from the inmates. They're usually ignored, but we have to read them. Or rather, you do. Human Rights and all that." She leafed through, quickly scanned one and placed it in front of him. "This one for example. Tidy, no obscenities, no dodgy stains. Some of them you won't want to touch, believe me. Ones like this need to be looked at, or we'd be in trouble. We

1

have some educated types here. So look at them all, but some you can chuck away without reading."

This was not getting better. Frank could see why the previous occupant had moved on, but asked her why anyway.

"Time for a change, I guess." Matilda said. "We liked Bill, sorry he went. So, do you know him?"

"No."

"Right. Anyway, go through the requests, log them all and pick out any that need action of some sort. Ignore defaced ones, threats, sob stories, whining – you'll get lots of that. Put the reasonable ones here," she tapped the corner of the desk, "and the rest down there." She pointed to the floor.

"Just on the floor?"

"Yes. Just there." She sensed his disapproval. "It's how it's done, so we all know what's what." Then she tapped the book. "You log everything in this."

There were other things. There weren't that many requests, so his time would be spent mostly logging assignments, transfers, punishments, general in and out stuff all of which routed through here, through the small desk in Room 33. Soon three trays were brought in, and four piles of papers overdue for logging. As they were dumped in front of him Frank was already on the verge of walking out. This job promised nothing but boredom and grief. He looked through the stack of papers and flicked through the log book, then spent a couple of hours trying to get into a suitable mindset. Then suddenly a small box with a chrome bell on the wall burst into life. He jumped. Moments later Matilda came in and pointed to the bell, as if Frank was unsure of where the noise had come from.

"That's the first exercise bell." She looked out of the window. "They'll be out in a minute. Three times a day – ten-thirty, two-thirty, six-thirty. Only for half-an-hour – it rings again when it's over. He wondered why such a loud bell was needed in the office, but didn't ask. Probably so they all know what's what. "Don't let those people bother you Frank. They can be distracting but don't fixate on it. I'd have blinds if it were up to me, but it isn't."

The view from the window was bleak. The square was an empty space some fifty metres each way, and surrounded by a four-metre fence that ran all the way around. There were two gates, one to the cells and another opposite that now opened. Six prison officers came out as a stream of dispirited-looking men appeared from the other side. The two gates closed, and suddenly the square came alive, or partly alive. A few were jogging around, but most wandered slowly around the perimeter, some talking, some lost in thought while the officers stayed in a safe huddle not far from their gate, watching. Frank counted thirty-two men moving around the fence.

"So are all these... murderers?"

"Yes," said Matilda, as she gave a little wave to the

officers across the square. Two of them waved back. "All killers of one sort or another. You wouldn't want to meet any of them, dark night or not."

Frank got up and stood at the window as the slow procession went past, five metres away.

"Must be grateful for the fence then," he said.

"Indeed." Then she turned away smartly. "But don't watch them, it makes them jumpy."

He sat down again and she left the room. He took a random sheet from the pile on the desk and looked it over half-heartedly, then he was drawn again to the scene outside his window. The procession kept moving, anti-clockwise, an inoffensive trail of criminals looking like people you would cheerfully say hello to if you didn't know them. *All killers of one sort or another.*

It was just after Matilda left him that it started. It was ten thirty-five, and the procession was in full swing. He found it fascinating to watch them, to guess why each man was there, to marvel at how some looked so harmless, so friendly. And what had they done? Were they all guilty of murder, or were some there for manslaughter? Earlier, he'd asked Matilda and she'd said, "No, all for murder. All premeditated." Then she'd warned him not to go by appearances. "You'll never get close to them anyway, but don't be fooled."

So he was watching off and on from his desk, and was suddenly aware of someone standing at the fence, a burly man dressed in a garish green and yellow boiler suit and in his late forties, perhaps, looking straight at him. Their eyes met, and the man's expression changed from benign to menacing, his eyes narrowing with a slight sideways lean of his head as he bared his teeth in a silent and threatening low-key snarl. Then his expression changed to a friendly smile as he looked straight at him, with his arms crossed. Frank looked away, but a minute later he was still there, unchanged as the line moved slowly behind him. And he was still there at eleven, when he was moved on by two of the officers. Frank was rattled. He went next door to Matilda.

"That's George," she said. "George Sweeney."

"Why does he look at me like that?"

"Well it's not love, believe me."

"Why is he doing it?"

"George is okay, just in a world of his own. You really have to live with him. Green and yellow means he's an escape risk, by the way – did you know that? They're talking about moving him to Category A. Anyway he won't stop while he thinks he's bothering you, so keep your eyes on your work. Never look out of the window. If he sees just a glance he'll know he's got you."

"Got me? So I can't look out of the window any more."

"No, not when they're out."

"That's impossible though."

"No it isn't," she said, "ignore him."

5

It was easier said than done. Frank would discover how hard it was to avoid looking at someone who's just there, outside your window, staring at you, so usually he would fail. His glance would be enough to encourage George. Such a friendly name though. But what was he trying to do? "Just intimidate you," Matilda said. "He doesn't need a reason."

But George did have a reason. He was unhappy with the man in Room 33. He stood by the fence and watched him twice a day as he sat at that desk sorting those papers, *signing* those papers that meant more problems for him. He was doing the same thing as Bill, the one he'd got rid of. It wasn't fair. Prison Officers – to George they were *screws* – would come into his cell with one of those papers and read it to him, and again he would be denied something. And for what? *This place is dog eat dog, so how can you blame me for defending myself?* Those screws attacked him three at a time whenever he was sorting someone out for them. There was no justice here, and that man at the desk was certainly someone who needed sorting out. It was obvious – stop him signing those papers and you stop George being victimised. So he stood there every time and waited for the man to look at him, which he always did, eventually – even facing away and swivelling his eyes to the side, but George was onto that. He'd got rid of the last one and he knew he was getting to this one. He would stop him signing those papers once and for all, and he knew how he would do it.

He'd explained the problem a week ago to his brother Dave, who was the only person to visit him, so far. This was when Bill was still there. George said through the grill to him, "I've decided Dave. There's a door, goes out from the corridor by the cells and it's on the same side as that room he's in. It's not far so I reckon it must join up somewhere. I'll get through there. I'll get him."

Dave was seriously alarmed. "George! They'll put you in Broadmoor! Don't be stupid!" Then he thought for a moment. "Anyway, how can you do that?"

George leaned closer to the grill, lowering his voice and looking shiftily to right and left. "I'll get the key off old Dennis. Piece of cake."

Dave leaned in close. He was whispering now.

"Who's Dennis?"

George nodded towards the door. "That's him over there. Too doddery for this job. I'll have the key in a jiff. Put him to sleep for a bit!" He smiled at the thought.

Dave, ten years younger, admired his big brother and was easily led to his way of thinking. He was streetwise but not the brightest. He would await developments. He went after a while, and George was left sitting there looking glum and unhappy in his green and yellow outfit.

: : :

"He's there again, Ma'am."

This was Frank's third morning. Matilda looked up from her work, and sighed loudly.

"Oh, Frank. Of course he is. Just don't look at him."

"Can't they move him on though, stop him looking at me? He just stands and stares."

"No. It's all they can do to get him back in his cell."

"What about curtains, or a blind? He's really bothering me."

"Get over it please."

"Can't I pay for some curtains then?"

"No you can't. Get over it."

End of conversation.

Frank's first three days were a time of mind-numbing boredom clearing the backlog and of getting used to the system, the bell still making him jump and one particular inmate giving him creepy looks. He really didn't think he'd last long. And he was overworked – he'd need to be there seven days every week to get it all done, but all he had was five, so Mondays promised to be work-heavy. And he was learning about people, hearing the gossip at the coffee machine, having to sit with whoever in the canteen because he was new. On his second day he'd heard something he wished he hadn't heard. It seems Bill didn't want a change. He was fired because he couldn't hack it.

Frank was in the canteen, next to someone he didn't

know. Early twenties, much like himself, friendly, and they got on well after the initial sussing out. This was Gary, from Reception, who said his job was easy compared to Frank's.

"How do you mean?"

"Well that last guy left in a bit of a state, didn't he."

"Did he? You mean Bill?"

"Oh, sorry – you didn't know... did you?" Then Gary told him all about it. All that he knew, anyway. Apparently Bill was given an ultimatum: get over it, or go. Something clicked in Frank's head, because that's the way he feared he was already going with Matilda. And Gary knew all about George's fixation. Everybody did. It was a joke to most of them but with poor Bill it became serious. He really couldn't cope with it.

: : :

Three weeks earlier...

Matilda sat on the late bus looking through the window at the wet pavement and the garish reflections of the shopfronts. The bus moved off, and as it went she saw an elderly man with a small bag tucked under his arm come from a dark alleyway and turn smartly alongside; he put his head down, but not before he'd looked straight at her. He couldn't hide the shock in his face, and she kept staring at him, looking back as the bus left him behind. Something about him was familiar, but she couldn't place him.

Next morning she sat eating breakfast and listening to the local news. The theft had just been discovered, breaking news, reporter at the scene, etc. It was at Timson's. The bus had stopped outside, and she'd been on board last night as that man came out of the darkness, out of the alley that led nowhere except the side door of the place. It was blank walls except for that door. She knew because the alley was familiar, from a hurried affair a year ago in Phil's car the night before he'd left her. It was perfect then, dark, dead-end, private. And she remembered who the man was. It was Colin Sweeney, George's uncle. She knew him from a chance meeting at the court where George was being tried. She'd been hanging around waiting for someone involved in another case, when he'd literally bumped into her as he was going in to plead for his nephew George.

"Oops darling - sorry!" he'd said, having a good look at her in the process. He wasn't beyond a bit of flirting, in spite of his age. And now she'd seen him coming away from Timson's with a bag under his arm. She didn't need Sherlock for this one.

She mulled it over, as if it were a moral question, as if there was something else she should do apart from report him. That was because she knew about George's family – if he'd recognised her things could become awkward. Dangerous, even. So she went to work, undecided, and as she walked up to the prison her fears were confirmed. It was Sidney, another uncle, who was waiting for her.

"Hello Matilda," he said, "you don't know me, but I'm George Sweeney's uncle." They stood together on the pavement. "It's a bit delicate, but my brother Colin is concerned about you. Any idea why?"

There was no way she could walk away from him.

"No. You tell me."

Sidney smiled. "Well, we're a bit worried you might say something about him that could get him into trouble. You with me now?"

The moment of truth. She could go either way. She stood in front of him, trying to weigh things up as he smiled at her.

After a few seconds he said, "No need to worry love, no need at all." He waited for her, but still she was quiet. "There's two ways of doing this Matilda," he said, "there's the easy way, and there's the hard way. Hard for you, anyway."

Then he said, "There's an envelope in my pocket. Now I could give it you and everything would be okay, or you could refuse and be looking over your shoulder for the rest of your life. What d'you think?"

A few more seconds of silence as she looked at him.

"Five grand in that envelope Matilda."

Five thousand pounds. She needed time to think, but

she didn't have time.

"Don't be stupid now," he said, "there's no risk to you – unless you walk away from me, that is."

Complete turmoil in her head, but she had to decide. So she decided. The envelope went discreetly into her bag, and that was that.

In the days after she was a mess, in her head. She'd taken a bribe, and she could easily imagine being called out over it. *Prison Office Manager, position of trust, complete betrayal, etc.* She imagined facing the judge – the shame, the looks from her colleagues. She saw it all, but could do nothing. And what if "the family" came to her again, for more favours? But as the days passed she calmed. All was quiet regarding Colin, and there was no evidence at the scene pointing to anyone, apparently. She would have to carry on. The five grand was very useful though.

She knew George Sweeney was a career criminal, and a psychopath, or so the police psychiatrist had said at his trial. *Psychopath.* The very word was frightening, but Matilda had met them before. Cruel, deceptive, complete absence of conscience or empathy. No cure, no treatment that worked. She knew never to be alone with people like that, and she knew the danger with George. Just as well he was always locked away. He had a long record of violence, but this was the culmination of it all – the murder of a security guard, easy, without thought, so now he's here for life. And he wasn't happy, but not for the obvious reasons. He hadn't been here long but already someone was upsetting him, someone in that room that looked out over the square.

His distorted mind had centred on Bill Warwick, a young bloke who had it in for him. George was giving him the treatment but still he was there every day, looking back at him then reporting on him. He worked it out, and it was obvious.

Things were tough for George. Complaints, aggravations, when all he was doing was looking after number one. It used to be nice walking around the square, meeting people, but really all he'd wanted was respect and some people didn't want to give it to him, so he'd had to remind them, and not so politely sometimes. Which meant trouble from the screws. That bloke in that room was always looking at him as he went round, then writing things down. He knew he was the one, so he was giving him the look every time now. No-one would walk with George any more because of him anyway. He had to go.

"It's him doing it, I know it is."

"Doing what, George?" This was Dave. It was visiting time.

George leaned forward and lowered his voice. They were almost nose-to-nose at the mesh.

"Listen. When I go out I see him in that room. He's always there, with papers and stuff. He's signing things, and I know it's about me because next thing is I get a roughing-up, or I miss my games break. Or they mess up my food. It's not right. I saw him with somebody else in there once, and he pointed at me through the window."

A pause.

"Why would he pick on you George?"

"You tell me."

"So who is he? You got a name?"

"Bill something. And it's Room 33, I know that."

"How d'you know that?"

"Peter told me. He knows stuff, been here for nine years. And now they've put curtains up, so I can't see him but I know he's there. I want those curtains down Dave, I need to see what he's up to."

"They're not going to do that are they."

"I want those curtains down," he said, and there was no shifting him. "Sort it for me Dave. That Matilda woman is the one you need to see. She's here. I've seen her."

Dave knew she was there. She was the one they had on a string, so it should be easy. He left after ten minutes, and as he went he saw her by the gate. She was definitely the one Sid had paid off. He hung around outside then stood in front of her as she left, and introduced himself.

"George's brother," he said, "and I need a favour."

She tried to step around him but he stopped her with a cheeky hand on her chest. "It's not much of a favour love, and it might keep you safe, if you know what I mean." So she listened, and he was right, it wasn't much of a favour. "It means a lot to George... and that means I'll be happier as well. Matilda, isn't it? Be sensible, Matilda."

She couldn't ignore him. So next day she took the curtains down, saying that electricity shouldn't be wasted on lights while they were closed, which was ridiculous because most days the lights were on anyway. And that's exactly what had sent Bill on his way. He couldn't hack it after that.

: : :

So now Frank sat in Bill's place, still wondering how long he would last. It was a Monday, his second, but already it seemed like his twentieth. The afternoon break had passed, and he sat gazing through the window at the empty square. George had been there again for the full half-hour, like a bizarre statue staring at him with that gormless smile. Something had to be done or he'd go the same way as Bill, he was sure of that. He got up and went through to Matilda. She looked up at him with her usual heavy sigh.

"Frank. Everything okay?"

"No Ma'am, I really need to talk to you about George."

She almost shouted at him. "Get over it! Don't you want to work here? It's all part of the job, you know!"

He was bolder than he should have been. "But you don't have to look at him. I do."

She was cross now. "Well I think you should just move on, Frank darling. Go and stack shelves somewhere. You know, somewhere safe."

He stood looking at her, needing the pay but not so much the job anymore.

She looked back to her work. "So are you still working here, or not?"

"Could I turn my desk around then, so I don't have to look at him?"

"No! You cannot!" She was glaring at him. Then she lost it altogether. *"Look – just... clear off. You're fired. Go!"*

"This is so unfair, Ma'am."

"Don't call me Ma'am. You don't work here now. Get out."

So Frank left her, collected a few things and went.

Matilda sat there, fuming. *So now it's on me. Again. And it's Monday, so there'll be loads he hasn't done.* She sat thinking for a while, then calmed down. *Maybe it's for the best. I'll get someone better. No more babies.*

So it was down to Matilda, the one who gets things done. She spent a couple of hours sorting out Frank's desk, slowly warming to her task. She would replace him with someone stronger. These boys were obviously not up to it, so she would choose the next one herself. She couldn't expect Personnel to keep replacing people without good reason, and her reasons were private, so the next one must be the last. These things were in her head as she worked, and other distractions were kept at bay by her dedication, her focus – and at five o'clock she was still there. She glanced at the clock. Two hours and she would leave. Some days were so long, others went by easily, but today had become pleasurable – momentous, even. Things would get better now. She wrote quickly into the log, no wasting time. *That's how it's done.*

But then she missed something.

She missed the heavy door behind her opening slowly and noiselessly, and the quick, brutal movement that followed gave her no time to be shocked. The alarm sounded as Matilda's life ended, condemned by her preoccupation and the efficiency of George Sweeney – who realised the switch but was quite unable to stop himself, being the psychopath he was... but what a surprise for him, to see Matilda signing those papers instead!

Room 33 was vacant again.

It's a Mark 1 Mini, the one with the starter on the floor.

Outside: England, rain. Inside: Italy, Annie Lennox. Hot, very loud, hand tapping wheel. Blue sign blurs past – *Portsmouth, 16.* In good time. Ring on finger, just the one. Happy girl, on her way, she's leaving him. Portsmouth (can't wait), ferry to Caen, slow drive through France to the South, and on to Italy. Slow run, down to the sun.

Portsmouth, straight on.

But suddenly, out of nowhere – doubt, and panic. *What?* – takes next exit. *Waterlooville?* All change. Sleep on it, take the morning boat. Expensive night, not planned. Vivien lies in bed, thinks of tomorrow then dreams of Frank. No say in that. Motel breakfast, indecision and more coffee, but then – what if he's looking for me? *Of course he is. Get going.*

Frank Davies is not happy. His arm finds cold empty sheets, and his car is missing. Policeman on station duty is helpful, even at 5am, even after Frank has exposed himself re-tying his dressing gown, Paisley, size M.

"Now where did you say she went, Mr Davies?"

"Her mother's."

"What time would that have been?"

"I don't know. Half-eight or nine. I went to bed."

"Did she say she'd be very late?"

Frank is distracted. "What? No, she didn't say anything."

"And have you spoken to her mother?"

"Not at bloody five in the morning, I haven't."

"Try to keep calm, sir."

"Look," says Frank, "my car is gone, okay? I've walked here in the rain, my coat's in the car... do you know what time it is? I'm wet..."

"Right sir, *calm down now*. We'll check with your mother-in-law."

"She's not there."

"How do you know that?"

"Because I know she's not there. She must have walked back and taken the car. It's gone."

"Have you tried to contact her?"

"She's not answering. Called and messaged. Nothing."

"Right, let's have some details of the car."

Pen poised, but Frank drifts again.

"And her suitcase is gone."

"Oh!" Policeman perks up. "You sure of that, sir?"

Frank takes a deep breath, lets it out, stares beyond.

"She's taken my Mini. Austin Seven, Mark 1, 1963. Mint condition, fantastic paint job – did it myself."

"And what colour would that be?"

Voice trembles. "Daytona Yellow. Green, *Sage* Green velour interior. Walnut dash." Frank begins to shake. Fists tighten, stares like an idiot.

Long arm on his shoulder. "Let's sit you over here. Was she your wife, sir – I mean, is she... your wife?" Leads him across the room, like an old man.

"Fiancée." Sits down, calmer now, pathetic. "We were going to get married! No chance now. That's it. That's bloody it."

Policeman sighs. A pause.

"Registration?"

Frank stares ahead. "FD187."

Policeman pounces, eyebrows shoot up: "Ah! – personalised?"

Frank swivels his head, looks at him. Pride returns.

"Yes. Frank Davies, 18 - when I bought the car. Couldn't help the 7." Another pause.

"So... any idea where she may have gone?"

A longer pause; still looking sideways at policeman. Suddenly a light flashes on, onto a memory, a bad memory. Frank jumps. Policeman jumps. Frank's hand goes to policeman's arm - *ITALY! Always on about it!* He tells policeman. Policeman suggests waiting, after checking the obvious: mother-in-law, friends, hospitals; Frank not impressed. What about ferries? Interpol? He knows she's on her way, maybe too late.

Italy. Well not with my car, mate. No driving on the wrong side with *my* car. Must call Geoff.

6.45am drizzle, car park outside Waterlooville, facing Portsmouth, engine purring. She turns it off, and slumps. Looks again at phone, still on silent, still three messages sitting there, unread. He'll be mad with her. Thinks again about the car. *Stupid. You can't take it. He'll never let it go.* Closes eyes, wishes she'd left it for him, then remembers the first time driving it, so careful, Pride and Joy, just painted. In love then, she thinks, she with him and he with his Mini. But always careful with it, probably why he stuck with her. A fiancée for life, that was it... no more responsibilities, enough with the car. And her mother – what would she think? Not a lot. Shocked of course. Liked Frank – the son she never had, she said. Poor Frank, engaged and all that, full of hope for the future, and then this. *Well Mum, there's more for me. A whole world more.* Now she feels better. *But get going!* Turns the key, presses the starter.

Rather earlier morning drizzle, outskirts of Guildford. Frank tips unfinished coffee into the sink, lifts his hand to Geoff pulling up outside, grabs his keys, and leaves. Out of town on A3, south.

"Hope we find her," says Geoff.

"We'll find her," says Frank, "no worries."

He looks sideways across wet misty fields and wonders... *how could he ever replace her?* Then Geoff says, "Do you reckon she's gone already? On the boat?"

"Maybe. At least I'll be sure." Despondent. "Couldn't miss a car like that. They'll have a passenger list or something."

"What if she went to Poole though, or Newhaven?"

Shakes his head. "Portsmouth's closer."

A3 becomes A3(M) southbound. Determined now, to leave rain and Frank behind, but both stay with her. Vivien chases her dream as Frank chases his... she zooms past something, *someone*, familiar, staring from the hard wet shoulder. Does a double-take but it's gone. Blue sign, *Portsmouth, Ferries, left*. Three miles to go, no turning back, doing the right thing. Tries to think ahead, across the channel, to France, to Italy. *But that was Frank.*

Frank is very unhappy now. He's wet, and spray blows into his open mouth as Daytona Yellow Mini melts into Hampshire Grey Drizzle. Shock turns to rage, Frank turns to Geoff, tinkering under car bonnet – shouts "DID YOU SEE THAT GEOFF? DID YOU SEE IT?" Points down road with shaking finger, "MY CAR! MY MINI!"

Begins frantic little dance on the spot, still pointing.

Geoff looks up, comes over, wet. "Really?"

"YES! REALLY!" Tries to calm himself. Must think. Man of Action now. Gripping Geoff's arm, "Will it go?" Geoff says no, alas. "Right!" Walks off briskly towards Portsmouth, thumb up, looking back.

"No! It's a motorway! We'll phone for help – come on!"

But Frank is off and away.

Vivien is worried. The image of a moment is filling her

mind. It was definitely Frank. Puts foot down, but it's already down. Blue signs blurring –

EndofMotorwayFerriesFollowSigns

...he's here! ...but he's there, stuck. He's worked it out, not stupid, not entirely. Manic driving, follow signs. Thinks, *I'll have to wait, I know I will... that only happens in films - boat leaving, last one on. Why did I wait?* Stops outside terminal, gripping wheel, heart thumping. Quick reverse across road, wait, despair then double yellow... what the hell, tow it away. Pulls off ring, puts in ashtray. Leaves car quickly, keys and all, dashes through lines of waiting cars, dragging suitcase.

Tremors through the deck. *Normandie* is moving, she feels it. Breathing slows, oddly calm now. *But I was lucky.* The longest twenty minutes. Sees him then, running into the terminal like a mad thing, looking for her. Or the car. She can see it – he goes back out. He's found it, or someone has – she strains to see; ship swings slowly around, blotting out by degrees. She leans out. Car jumps forward, disappears behind lifeboat. Quickly through to the other rail, waiting, waiting, then small yellow car appears, moving slowly.

Arm out of window? *Yes.* Straight up, too far away to see... two fingers, perhaps just one – for her, of course. Arm goes in, window slides shut as he races away. Relief, elation. On her own, free to go, but suddenly there's sadness for things.

No going back, Vivien.

As she drifts towards the open sea the keys drop from her fingers, forty-five feet, straight down, gone – front door, coffee machine, stationery cupboard (send them a postcard).

Ahead of the ship, the sky clears.

THE WORLD ALONGSIDE US

The Lost Journal of 17 days,
December 2023 - January 2024

This journal begins Friday, December 29th 2023.

The world is empty of people, except for me. Yesterday I thought I heard a helicopter somewhere far away, but I was mistaken. I really think it's just me now, and the winter's becoming colder. A thin trace of snow sweeps my patio – it's too cold to stand out there, and the birds watch me from the thin branches, waiting to be fed.

Three days ago I woke to find myself alone in bed (not unusual), alone in the house (also not unusual), but seemingly quite alone in the world, at least the world I can reach from here. No sign of anyone. No bodies either. After three days I've stopped expecting to wake up from this.

Some background: My name is Jeffrey Carson, and I turned forty last September. I like to think I'm not easily scared, but what's happened has proved me wrong many times. I woke quite early on December 26th (Boxing Day, in the world as it was) and found myself to be completely alone. Wandered about for a bit. No power, no water, no phone, no sound, just the wind in the trees. Very eerie, couldn't make sense of anything. No lights anywhere down in town, no road noise coming up. Sat down in utter confusion. Worried for my wife. Where is Christine? Walked around the hill, to all our neighbour's houses. The friends I had were missing. I was alone with nature, with the trees and the birds, and now and then I panicked. This was like a parallel universe, and somewhere just out of reach was my old life with my wife and my friends. Am I dreaming this? Extreme confusion. Missed breakfast. Late morning I drove down – shops locked up, cars all over the place. Absolutely no signs of humanity, all houses I went into quite empty. Sat in the car, not knowing what to do. Went back up, felt better at home, in familiar surroundings. Made very late (cold) lunch. Very confused and tired so tried to sleep, thinking this would somehow put things right, but couldn't relax. Tried to think straight. After a few hours I went back down, in a daze, with list of essentials: bottled water, batteries, food and so on. Had to break into shops, felt very wrong but what else could I do? Took generator from hire shop, then remembered that water has stopped and none stored. Went to supermarket for loads more bottles. Already behaving like a lone survivor of some terrible event. Nobody stores petrol it seems, at least that I can access, so generator is diesel. Farmers have tanks of diesel. I'll need to borrow a diesel car.

Managed to sleep that night, but everything the same when I woke.

So that was then, and now, 3 days later, I slide in and out of despair. Keeping my phone charged, but it's just a camera now.

Yesterday drove to Ross, Hereford, Gloucester. The same everywhere I went, no people, but also no bodies. Roads difficult, strewn with vehicles. Back home kept several radios on, different wavelengths, nothing but static. TV dead, of course. Periods of panic, then incredible calmness and clarity. Slow realisation that this could be my life now.

I'm hoarding diesel, filling endless jerrycans, but it won't last for ever. Someday the car will stop, the generators (three of them now) will stop, and at least I'll get some peace. Then it's legs and candles and silence - back to nature, if I can call it that. No more music, no more static from the empty radio. How long? Food will be a problem, but I've brought up plenty of tins and dried stuff. I remember reading that tinned baked beans lasted fifty or sixty years. But that was in extreme cold, in the Antarctic. My freezers will stop sooner or later – dried food is good for maybe ten years, tins possibly the same. I'll have a vast stock of out-of-date food. It's been three days, and already I'm thinking of ten years!

Food will be the problem. And water, but there's the river below the hill. I'm no gardener so I must do some serious survival reading and think about growing veg. Internet would be very useful! Often wondered how we'd manage without it, so now I'll find out. Also I think it might be sensible to get a gun (end-of-the-world, hostile gangs wandering around, dystopia etc). Not sure where to look for one. But farmers have shotguns, surely. Three days, and already this feels permanent.

Saturday 30th Dec

There are so many things I can't understand. This house is not quite as it should be. There are differences. My books have strangers amongst them, and a stranger's clothes are mixed in with mine in the wardrobe, yet so much of it is as it was. The Christmas presents are here, the tree, even the remains of the cake. I can't explain any of it. My wife, my friends, where are they? I'm in a crazy world where nothing adds up. I'm confused, and wishing it were a soon-ending dream, waking again to my wife, to my people, my work, my life, everything as it was before this nightmare.

I stood on the patio today in the sharp breeze, and looked down at the town. I do this a lot, remembering the view as it was, with lights and movement, and the distant noise. The aspect is almost north-west towards the first far hills of Wales, over a dozen or more farms beyond the outskirts of the lifeless town.

Found a shotgun at the farm down the hill. Tried it out in the garden. Didn't do it right, so bruised my shoulder. Tomorrow I shall go on an outing with plenty of provisions, and drive towards London. I have to do this. I'll sleep in the car and go all over the city. There must be someone else. I can't be the only "survivor", if that's what I am (a survivor of what?) but I'll come back here to my hill no matter what. I feel safer here.

Tonight I'm thinking of deep things, before I sleep - I miss Christine, my best friend, my confidante. Where is she? Is she safe, or is she gone from me for ever? I think of friends and relatives, Australia, Switzerland, and closer. What's happening the other side of the world?

Sunday 31st Dec

This morning, first thing (6.15) – a light! Definitely, a light winked at me from across the hollow of the town, from somewhere on the low slope of the opposite hill. I couldn't move, but kept my eyes on the spot, still in darkness. Nothing more, but enough to throw me into a heart-thumping rush of panic. I knew I had to keep the exact point in my vision, but it wouldn't be light enough to see details for at least another hour. So I tried to photograph with my mind the faint edge of the hill against the sky, to preserve the image. I let it go, got the torch, and flashed across the void to what must be another human being. No response. As it became lighter, I could see the small cluster of farm out-buildings, about two miles away. A familiar view, but now very important. I found them on the map and set off, a little apprehensive. They were empty. No signs of anyone having been there, as lifeless as everywhere else. I covered the whole area for half a mile around. I didn't go to London today, but tonight I shall watch through the darkness for the light. Strong coffee instead of milkless cocoa! My spirits are high, because of a pinpoint of light that may show itself again.

Monday 1st Jan
2024 - a new year
I slept in daylight this morning, worn-out, depressed. No light, unless I missed it, unless I imagined it yesterday anyway. Everything the same. Writing this in Central London, in sight of Big Ben, who doesn't chime any more. THERE IS NOBODY. The trip down the M4 was bizarre. Came past Bristol, Swindon, Reading – hundreds of cars, lorries, coaches, all abandoned, stretching the whole length. Heathrow silent, lots of Marie Celeste half-eaten meals. Why are there no CRASHED cars? Or planes? Everyone's been spirited away so neatly.
Sleep in the car tonight, and look for a powerful transmitter/radio sort of thing in the morning. Is anybody out there?

Tuesday 2nd Jan
10.50pm. Back home, the mystery deepens. Someone's been here. Got back about 4, as the daylight began to fade, and didn't notice anything amiss but later, after dark, as I went to start the second generator I saw the side gate was open. I never leave it open. Very scared about this. Went back inside and locked all the doors

and windows and haven't been out since. The little generator will run out of fuel soon, and the house will be in darkness. I hope that whoever was here (still is here?) is friendly. When I thought I was alone, it was easier but now I could have enemies. I think I'll be braver in daylight. Still, setting the alarm for five to watch for that light again.

Wednesday 3rd Jan

No light first thing, and no more signs of anyone near the house. Crept out toting the shotgun like Clint Eastwood and scouted around, but nothing to suggest another person apart from the open gate. Nothing has really changed, the world looks the same. This is beyond bizarre.

Managed to sleep eventually last night, filled with anxiety about my possible/probable "visitor". Woke before the alarm. Spent the morning setting up my new radio and scanner. I can send messages on one and listen on the other. Very expensive, but free for me. Lots of batteries. I'm sending messages every 15 minutes and leaving the scanner on, but nothing so far. So many frequencies apparently, a new world for me. Very lucky if I hit on one that works. I'm also recording everything – I don't want to miss anything, so I spend hours listening to emptiness. Apparently my messages could be picked up all over Europe. Anyone listening?

Sat on the patio again after lunch, quite warm in the

sun. I think I'm coping with all of this quite well, but I still panic sometimes. The fear of the unknown, and of my visitor yesterday. The isolation, and the thought of being totally alone in the world, and therefore vulnerable to whatever comes along, in whatever shape or form. Making plans for survival (the strongest urge, of course) isn't difficult. Food can be grown, water can be saved, and life can proceed without electricity. I just wonder about how hard I should try, to contact others in the world? Maybe it's better as it is. All the old films about starting again after Nuclear devastation or whatever, end with power struggles and violence – someone has to be the boss, it seems. Perhaps I shouldn't light up the house. What fears I have!

I need to store water, so tomorrow I'll look for a water tank – I could die for a hot bath, but still I'm loathe to waste that much water.

Suddenly it hits me that yesterday's visitor must have been here in the early evening, while I was inside. The gate was shut when I got home, I'm certain.

Thursday 4th Jan

Tonight I'm in my car, writing by torchlight. I'm going to sleep here, near the buildings where I saw the light again this morning. It winked twice to me, the second time fading slowly to nothing, and I'm certain of the source – the stone barn 200 yards ahead, which is empty. I have the slight security of the car around me, and I have the shotgun, but I'm nervous. Darkness these days holds different fears than before, and possibilities are everywhere. Feeling brave, but I'm scared.

Not much else to report from today: found a water tank, but needs to be filled! Loads of bottles of water going up the hill. It's beginning to snow, very gently.

Friday 5th Jan

Home. I've entered a sort of fantasy-world, after last night. I slept, without meaning to, in the car for (I think) about two hours, waking this morning at nearly seven. It was light, overcast and snowing. I was annoyed for not watching through the night, and for missing the light. I got out of the car, looked all around and was about to walk up to the barn when it struck me that the marks and ruts in the snow on the lane hadn't been there when I arrived. I suppose I expect farm lanes to be muddy, and rutted with potholes, but this lane was tarmac, I was certain. I scraped with my boot and found the smooth surface below. The snow was just an inch thick, and only began falling after I arrived last night. I admit to being badly frightened. The tracks in the snow – footprints, wheel ruts or whatever they were – covered the whole width of the lane. Many comings and goings within inches of the car. Who were these people? Why didn't I hear them? And where are they now? After looking in real horror at the marks and seeing them trailing off into the distance towards the barn, all thoughts of making contact had gone. The snow was turning to rain and I came straight home, after seeing the tracks disappear before reaching the beginning of the lane. Where they came from, I've no idea. Not brave enough to follow the traces. A big mistake. I should have followed them but it was the amount of activity that scared me.

The day's been spent moving stuff around, making the house more secure. I feel more safe during daylight, as if it were vampires that bothered me. It's very depressing, the thought that I'm really afraid of something unknown.

Saturday 6th Jan

Worked hard all day on the house in a sort of desperation, and I didn't look for the light this morning – I'd rather ignore it now. So I'm here, in a house becoming a fortress and always in fear of someone or something appearing around a corner. I cannot be calm. The windows are shuttered and everything I need is locked up, including the generators. I have four now. And a huge amount of diesel. I'll still need to leave the house though, to get to my various sheds and the garage, but I don't like the dark. And I'm afraid that walls and barriers won't be enough to stop these people if they choose to pay me a visit. I keep the shotgun loaded and close to me. The snow is disappearing.

I've been thinking seriously of leaving. Perhaps I could set up again far away from here – when the snow has gone though, so I need a weather forecast. I could go wherever. It sounds as though I'm on the run. Wish I could calm down. No explanations for what's happened, but how, and why, did they miss me? AND WHO ARE THEY? If only a human being would knock on my door.

Sunday 7th Jan

Last night, noises around the house. Just after midnight, the big locked shed door was opened (unmistakable sound) and soft footfalls on the gravel under my bedroom window. Then, the front door handle was tried, gently and quietly. Had the gun ready, peeped from the window, saw nothing, nobody. Too terrified to go down. This morning nothing is amiss outside, apart from the UNLOCKED and opened shed door. Decided to find a night camera today, but then –

A BREAKTHROUGH!

A message from someone, somewhere, came through early this morning, before I was awake. My breakfast routine is to listen to the night's recordings, fast-forwarding and listening for anything apart from the static. It was there, halfway through. After hours of background hiss came a man's voice, in a light French accent, fading in and out – a message telling me and anyone else to go to Limoges, in France:

"Seventh January. Transmission Europe. Use frequency nine point five megaherz repeat nine point five. First live contact at Limoges France repeat Limoges France. Safe area Sardinia repeat Sardinia. Use main roads only. Do not travel in darkness. Stay on main road, stay in locked vehicle sunset to sunrise, you will be safe. Leave immediately..."

There were contact details for Limoges, then after a moment the message played again, but in Italian. So I'm not alone! Sardinia is apparently "safe", but safe from what? Or who? Also do not travel in darkness. Suits me. I will go. Wish I could drive through the Channel Tunnel but that's for trains, so I must be a sailor, and find another car the other side. At least I found most abandoned cars have their keys. Keys but no drivers.

I spent hours packing, aware that I may never return. Christine was the packer par excellence, so I took forever, obsessing over what to take. Why did I say she WAS? Ended up with one smallish suitcase, minimal clothing, spare shoes, boots, maps, money (for what?), the scanner/transmitter and batteries, and my phone charger – forever hopeful! Left just after ten and headed for Dover, the shortest route across for a non-sailor like me. Took a neighbour's Range Rover as I expected some off-roading to get around the car-chaos. 2.30pm, looking at the sea. Calm, not much wind but I won't go today. Found a boat with an engine. No sails, thank you. Found the Marina and wandered the jetties, looking for something sensible, and there it was: La Belle France. How could I resist? Lovely solid little cabin cruiser, tidy and hopefully well maintained. Spent half an hour working out how to start the engine, then another hour reversing out and tootling around the Marina. Ready! All went well, but "do not travel in darkness" bothers me, so I've parked up by the jetty and locked myself in the car. The message told me I'd be safe in here, so I'll reluctantly trust it and try to sleep.

Monday 8th Jan
Uneventful night, slept better than feared. Breakfast at 7.30, orange juice and dry crackers, tinned fruit. Limoges, halfway down France, here I come! Bitterly cold, but no snow left now and everything's ready. Towing a small inflatable dinghy with an outboard motor, just in case. 27 miles, so I reckon two hours max to Calais.

Tuesday 9th Jan
11.45am Parked just before Paris, on the Autoroute south. Empty cars everywhere. Remembered to put my watch an hour ahead, but does that matter any more? The crossing yesterday was interesting, to say the least. What looked easy was not, but after THREE hours I got into Calais. Needless to say, the satnav on the boat was dead, so I thought all I had to do was follow the compass heading. Big mistake. Not a clear day. Very windy so blown down the Channel without realising how far, and of course the heading was different from there. Eventually

found the coast somewhere south west of Calais, then followed it back until the harbour breakwaters appeared. Found a car with keys and a full tank, just managed to start it. Made coffee with a little gas stove liberated from a Carrefour superstore en route. So much stuff I could have taken, but settled for camping gear, clothing, a few tools. Decided to get a handgun. Feel stupid walking around with the shotgun, but kept it in the car. Found a gun shop in Calais and took a 9mm Colt and lots of ammunition. Handsome, deadly thing. No idea what I'm afraid of but felt a bit more secure, especially after firing it into a tree a few times. Hope I never need it. This place is so empty.

Wednesday 10th Jan

So much has happened. Yesterday, at 90km from Limoges I pulled over and listened for "a live contact" on a certain wavelength, as the first message had told me to. Nothing for a few minutes, then the same recorded voice as on that first message gave me directions into the city, to an underground car park. There was a camera on the wall, and the gates opened for me and I drove into the semi-darkness. There were cars neatly parked. The gun was in my lap. Followed the arrows, and then, in my headlights, a figure came out and stood against the end wall, waving to me. You cannot imagine how I felt. I had no idea if this person would harm me, but I was elated. Death could have come at that moment, but still I was elated. The figure motioned me into a space and walked towards me. Death or salvation. I lowered the window, and a friendly-looking Frenchman held his hand out to me and said Bonjour. I said Hello as I shook his hand through the window. This was Laurent. You won't need the gun, he said.

He was one of a group of five who are there to manage the arrivals and send them on to Sardinia. They are two women and three men, all nationalities, and all friendly and capable. They live underground, in the vast car park, in converted store rooms and the like. I slept in a cubicle and felt properly safe for the first time in many days. They have a vast stock of food and are very organised, and luckily for me their English is good. Each of them had a disturbing story to tell, of being badly frightened by something they never actually saw. Early this morning they told me what would happen on my journey south, and when we left the sun was warm through the windows of the minibus. There were three of us plus Pete, the English driver, and we had to reach the port of Toulon before dark. Pete was chatty. We asked him so many questions. The beefy Norwegian guy next to me wanted to know what the dangers were if we travelled in darkness.

Pete said they have a friend called Fabrice who tested the danger. We'd meet him on the island. He left the bunker without telling anyone and stayed in his car on the Autoroute outside Limoges, all locked up, then at midnight he drove away, but within one minute he'd stopped again, after seeing something up ahead. Pete laughed at brave Fabrice being scared. The "something" came towards him then disappeared. It was darker than the night, Fabrice said, but what it was, he didn't know. He came back in the morning.

Two people have disappeared from the Limoges bunker in the past months, simply gone from their beds in the night. Again, a mystery. Pete said there must be many millions gone throughout Europe. The original Limoges team had a few disappearances as they converged on the city.

The bunker was started six months ago. Laurent was one of the originals, and the car park was chosen because of the human need to hide away from danger, but it's apparently no safer than being on the surface. Daylight is reckoned to be safe, because (so far) all disappearances and vague "encounters" have happened in darkness. No record of anyone actually being harmed though, just badly frightened, so the real threat is unknown. Another thing: helicopters. They have two, but just one (barely-qualified) pilot. He's been criss-crossing Europe on the off-chance of seeing someone, so maybe I did hear one. He found no-one in the whole of London, nor Paris, apparently. Not one person. Been doing it for months and they've worked out fuel supplies but I guess it won't last for ever.

And I asked Pete why Sardinia was chosen. He didn't know, but people wanted out of the bunker and felt safer on an island, with the sea around them. No protection really but it felt better in the sunshine, and in the five months since only three people have gone from there. So comparatively safe. And the island is welcoming, and fertile.

The crazy thing is that the people who vanished from the mainland and the few from Sardinia had already been "disappeared" from wherever they originally were, so where did they go this time? Back to where they came from? Too much for my puny brain. Nils, the Norwegian, agreed: "A shift in the natural order of things," he said, "that our brains cannot work out" (you can say that again) and Hanne, the Danish woman the other side of me said maybe we'll never return.

Happy thoughts indeed, while I wondered what would happen if Pete the driver suddenly disappeared – but apparently we need darkness for that.

Thursday 11th Jan

2.30pm. I'm here on Sardinia, sitting on a bench overlooking the harbour at Porto Torres. It's pleasant, but not warm, and the sky is cloudless. Arrived an hour ago on a hydrofoil, and 5+ hours at around 55mph was exhilarating! Pete dropped us at the harbour in Toulon yesterday and we joined eight others who'd waited several days for us. Left there after a good breakfast this morning. Given food when we arrived here and shown our quarters, but really we can choose to wander the island if we wish to, and find somewhere else to stay. Seven communities here, living off the land in a sort of doomsday scenario where nobody feels really secure. Hotels and private houses are used, and everyone is more or less happy to help with providing. No talk of "personalities" or cult-leaders yet. Just a matter of time though, I guess. Lots have crossed the 8 miles to Corsica. A good estimate of population is 325, allowing for disappearances, which should always be reported to HQ at Porto Torres. Thankfully there are doctors here.

This was an island of 1.6 million people, now all vanished. There's no shortage of places to sleep so I shall stay here in Porto Torres, I think. I look back at pictures from home on my phone, of Christine, of the garden and all around, and wonder if I'll see them in reality again. I'm also taking pictures, but only out of habit.

I wonder, is this madness? Is this how it feels? Have I imagined or dreamt all this? How will it end? Will I live out my days here, or will I just vanish one dark night and end up somewhere else, to start all over again? All impossible to answer.

Friday 12th Jan

Exactly two weeks since I woke up at home, and began this bizarre adventure. I'm told people arrive every week on the hydrofoil and very occasionally by helicopter, but no-one leaves the same way. The realists among us await our turn to disappear, but no-one here has been physically harmed it seems, just confused and frightened. It's a very odd existence.

Talking with people is interesting. So many opinions, so many differences in response to all this. Some convinced of aliens, some of time warps and parallel universes – a world alongside the one we knew – but many terrified and never far from tears. Hanne, the Danish woman, is convinced of an alien presence. Definite signs of beings moving about, but no real sightings from anyone apart from Fabrice's scary encounter. So was it an alien that opened my gate? And my shed? And lots of them passing my car as I slept? Invisible things? If we could see what or who we're dealing with it would be less frightening. Or maybe not. And ALIENS does not explain leaving one life for another. What happened that first night? The world is certainly upside-down.

Met the aforementioned Fabrice this morning. He's a friendly guy. He's tidied up an old tumbledown shack and opened a café of sorts, with fruit juices and offerings from his alcohol stash, and various dried foods and tins he's picked up. And on Tuesday evenings he brings out a guitar and sings, apparently. There's plenty of food here, and a surprising amount of optimism regardless of the loss we all feel.

Saturday 13th Jan

So much for optimism. Writing this late in the evening,

after a strange day of intense longing for my old life. I could weep. The doors and windows are closed and locked against the imagined threat, and I almost wish I could vanish from this new life and take my chances elsewhere.

Sunday 14th Jan

Cycled round part of the island today, 50 miles or so, but unable to raise my spirits much higher than a detached interest in what should be a fascinating place. So much beauty, but I need to sleep. I miss Christine. I look at her picture on my phone, whenever I feel like taking more. This journal will dry up, as I fear my life will.

: : :

I was alone in bed when I woke. It was Friday, Boxing Day, and Christine had left early for her morning's work and as usual was successful in not disturbing me. I lay awake and the memory rushed in like a tidal wave and engulfed me. I'd been away for more than two weeks. But was I really home? Christine's side of the bed was slept in, the duvet turned back. I reached for my phone and the date was confirmed. It was Friday December 26th, the same morning I'd woken to sixteen days before in a different world. I went downstairs to my breakfast things laid out for me on the kitchen table.

I spent the morning taking stock of my life.

My journal had gone, no new pictures on my phone. I would have to tell Christine. It wasn't a dream, nor was it imagined, and I knew I would have to share it with someone. I couldn't just get over it and carry on, so when she walked in just before lunch I rushed over and hugged her tightly. She almost lost her balance.

"I must tell you something. You'll think I'm insane."

I sat her down next to me at the kitchen table. After a deep breath I told her that on Boxing Day I'd woken up without her and there was no-one else anywhere. Nothing added up, the world was different. I told her I was scared and barricaded the house, and days later had a message to go to Limoges, and Sardinia, and I spent two weeks and a couple of days away before waking up without her missing me. She was silent and I was embarrassed, but she just looked kindly at me. There were tears in her eyes.

"This is such a relief Jeffrey, you've no idea."

Confusion, all over again.

She reached for my hand. "Well... I also went to Sardinia, last September." I stared at her. "I was terrified of telling you, in case you thought I was mad. I imagined you telling me it's just some super-realistic dream."

I was genuinely struck dumb.

She went on, "Anyway it was the same for me, no people anywhere. The first day I sat outside and watched the birds. It was still warm, long days and evenings. Then I went down to town and found a generator, a little one, enough for a few lamps, to boil the kettle, charge the torch, charge my phone. Then early one morning I heard a helicopter long before I saw it, and it saw me frantically waving the torch. Landed on the lawn, would you believe? No time to pack, really." She looked through the window. "Landed just out there. So I was taken away. We picked up four others near Limoges, then flew on to Sardinia. And three weeks later I woke up next to you, as normal. But it was all too much to talk about then, without you thinking I was crazy. I thought I'd never see you again." We hugged each other, sitting at that kitchen table.

I said, "I wrote a journal, pages and pages of it."

She said, "So did I. Pages and pages. And photographs. All gone."

She saw some of the Limoges people on the island. Certainly she knew Fabrice. And met Laurent, briefly. She came back in the night the same way I did. None of the pictures we'd taken came back with us, but our memories did, and we wondered about telling others. We would be laughed at. We decided to say nothing, at least until we'd come to terms with what had happened. So much in our lives now is unexplained. And we both wanted to go back to the lovely island in the Mediterranean.

After much looking-forward, in late March we travelled

again to Sardinia, this time flying to Alghero and taking a taxi to Porto Torres. We planned to return on the ferry to Toulon, hire a car and drive up to Limoges to check out my bunker. We went all over and found the places we remembered, and the houses we'd slept in, all filled with families and tourists now. The island looked much the same. Interestingly, Fabrice's little café was still the shanty it was before he rebuilt it.

Then, at the end of our week, and after tea with some Brits who were staying on, we walked down in the early evening with our suitcases to the harbour to take the ferry. We hadn't really noticed there weren't many people around. We'd just gone through the harbour gates when a guy came up to us and asked what we were doing. We said going home, and he said, "You won't get anybody to take you. It's not safe anywhere else, you know that."

We just looked at him, then, for a long moment, at each other. Around us the harbour was almost deserted, just a few people here and there. The sea was calm, unchanging. There was no ferry waiting.

"The other day I had an idea. When you live alone you have ideas, unless your head is empty or filled with rubbish like Mrs J next door who sits all day in front of the TV which I can hear through the wall and complains of how things are so different from when she was a girl. Well Mrs J, I want to say to her, that's what you get by listening to people with less in their heads than you, but I can't do it. She wouldn't listen to an old man anyway. Especially this one. I just feel sorry for her. Her daily waddle to the corner shop is her only trip to the outside world, and every day is like the last one. And the same goes for the millions stuck to their phones or laptops or whatever, who think they're in touch with things that matter. I feel sorry for Mrs J.

"Anyway, I had this idea. Living alone is good and bad, if you like people. It's good because you get a break from the annoying ones, and bad because you don't want to lose the good ones. But if you don't like people, you're laughing. I miss people. The ones I grew up with are all gone and, well, I'm an old man now - all I've got are memories and photographs. But there are people who call in, to be honest. There's the postie – they chop and change, male or female, you never know. They usually have time for a chat. They never chat with Mrs J though because she can never get there in time, and that's her own fault. I'm always there for them. Then there's Steve from the Community Centre, who pops in once a week unless he's away somewhere. I see him twice a week at the Centre but he checks on me anyway as if I can't look after myself, but he's a kind person. Tomorrow's his day, I think.

"Anyway, I had this idea. The postie brought me a new phone book. We chatted about how we don't get the big ones any more, just the little local ones like this one. We're all supposed to go online these days, or text people or email them. I still write letters. Anyway, I sat down with this little book and flipped through it. There were so many firms in there, hundreds I think, and that meant hundreds of people, at least. And I thought, what if some of those people are lonely? Of course they go out to work every day but you can be lonely in a crowd, can't you. For instance, on page five was Cats Are Love, which sounds strange, but what they do is look after cats while their owners are away. Full board for cats! And I wondered about the people who look after them. If they get their love from cats, maybe they need that because they're lonely otherwise. Just a thought. I had all these people in front of me, and some of them must be lonely. So my idea was to ring a few numbers, introduce myself and chat a bit, you know, put them at ease, sound them out. You soon work out who's needy and who's not.

"So I started from the front with ABC Cabs but that was a pain because the girl just kept asking me where I wanted to go. I said I don't want to go anywhere, but she didn't get that. Then she said she was busy, so I had to let her go. I didn't try her again. As I said, you soon work out the needy ones. So the first day was a bit frustrating. There was only one hopeful, a man from the old folks' home up the road which I'd rung by accident, but I'm glad I did, really. He was happy to chat, but a bit too happy actually, so after about half an hour I had to tell him I was busy. So the first page was a bit patchy, well, very patchy if I'm honest. Apart from the old bloke in the home, who wasn't needy, only bored I reckon, there was just one woman who sounded nice and chatted for a minute or two until I heard another voice say something and we were cut off. I rang back straight away but she didn't pick up. I'll try her again sometime.

"Steve came around next morning, and was interested in my little scheme. He's a very caring person. He asked me about it and wanted to know all the details, who I was ringing, what we talked about and so on. Then he said I should be careful because you never know who might get the wrong idea and try and rob you! I said that won't happen but he was concerned, all the same. He wants me to take another test. I did one a few months back and passed with flying colours he said, so no need to worry, but now it's time for another one. I'm not bothered. Remembering numbers and stuff is easy, and I only need to get some of it right apparently. He'll let me know when.

"The next day I skipped a few pages and landed on

the Cs which is where I found the cats one, but the girl there was a bit stroppy when I rang her back. I thought she'd dropped the phone or something, it went off so quickly. So I tried a few in Catering, then skipped Cemeteries and Crematoriums and tried Computer Repairs. They're a funny lot though, asking me why I was ringing if I didn't even have a computer. I said I wanted a chat, and anyway what if I wanted to buy one? And they said look on amazon, which was a mystery.

"Anyway the upshot of all this is that I have quite a few new friends, and I know it should be me who says sorry, wrong number because sometimes I get it wrong but a lot of the time it's the person the other end says it, so that's why I ring them again, because it's not a wrong number at all. But to be honest I rang a funeral director once when it should have been one of my florists, but he sounded so dour I was glad when he said he didn't have time. Some people I have to ring a few times before they speak to me, but I reckon they're not the needy ones. The needy ones will talk, but sometimes even the most lonely ones won't chat for long. This morning I spoke to Janice again, but she was too busy, she said. I'm pretty sure about her though. I don't know if she lives alone - she kept saying she lives with someone - but I think she does live alone. I spoke to her again this morning.

"Steve means well but he came in yesterday and said you've left the cooker on but why would I do that? And he's worried about my phone bill! And he asks me daft

questions like am I taking my tablets. I don't need them
but of course I am. If I miss one I take two next day.
He checks me on that. I wish he'd stop confusing me.
He said he came in last week but he didn't. And he says
maybe I'd be better if I lived somewhere else, but why
would I want that? And all this nonsense about tablets.
I take two the next day. What's the problem? He knows
I don't need anything as I get to the corner shop most
days, and I have a wide circle of friends now since I
started ringing people. And I've had a new idea.
Because a lot of my numbers don't connect any more
I've started making up numbers and ringing them.
Usually, to be honest, they don't work either but
sometimes someone answers and I can have a little
chat. I don't know who they are but it must be dozens
now. Had one in Africa the other day! Strangers,
enjoying a little talk with someone, and this is what the
world needs. Real connections, not people on key-
boards. When I started I used to think I was lonely, but
not now. To be honest I get a bit confused with
numbers sometimes, but I'll keep on talking to people
because I like being helpful if I can. And now Steve
wants to pop in twice a week, something about making
sure I'm not short of anything. And tomorrow he's
bringing someone very special with him he said, so
that'll be nice."

Phillip Barensson stood in the milling crowd at the top of the Campanile, striving for a glimpse of the city from a viewpoint he'd not visited before. The whole of Venice was laid out from the four sides of this fabled tower, and his visit was the resolution of a promise made to himself many years before, to come to *La Serenissima* again and view her from this perfect height. He spent ten minutes going from side to side politely jostling for position - Venice in the summer is always busy - and finally won himself a place on the west side overlooking St Mark's Square, resolving to hold it against all comers.

The view was sublime on such a day, the deep blue of the sky fading paler into white and gold over the distant islands, far beyond the city stretched out all around him. Then, as he looked down into the square, the first thing that caught his eye amongst the scattering of people far below was a man with a backpack and carrying a red bag, and Phillip was intrigued for no apparent reason except that this man stood out as he strode through the square. He walked faster than the others, who were more intent on loitering, perhaps, and the pigeons scattered from his path as he went. It was a few seconds, that's all, then he was gone from view, but something of this striding figure stayed with him, and interested him enough to make him give up his space. He squeezed his way back through the throng, made his way down from the tower and stood in the heat of the square, looking in the direction of the man with the red bag. He'd gone, of course, but he wondered what had put the image of him so well in his brain that he wanted to find him again. A man with a bag, like hundreds in Venice that afternoon, but such a *red* bag, and such an interesting urgency about its owner.

Phillip Barenssen was a writer by trade, with forty-three years' experience of life and with some reputation as a storyteller, so as his mind turned he began to muse on possibilities, to think that perhaps all was not well with this man. He was striding, after all, and who strides so urgently through St Mark's Square? Who would be so oblivious to the beauty around him? Well, maybe he was simply eager for his tea, but Phillip was a storyteller and the urge had arrived to find him and to build upon him.

: : :

Steven Barensson was indeed looking forward to his tea. He unlocked the door to his apartment in Calle Dei Albanesi, hung the key beside the door and went into the kitchen, putting his red bag onto the worktop and his backpack carefully onto the small table against the wall. It had been a good day for him so far, and he saw no reason for his luck to change.

He was a dealer in antiques who fancied himself an expert in glassware, and Venice is famous for its glassware. Murano, the island almost a mile to the north, was known throughout the world as a centre of excellence, and Steven Barensson was known as a man of some integrity and one to be trusted in the matter of fine glassware, at least by those who had no expertise in the subject. He was reckoned by most to be fair, and who in truth can expect more than fairness?

Today he'd found a trove of small, exquisite beads, fifteen of the finest examples of late seventeenth-century glasswork from the furnaces of Ferro Murano, one of the oldest and most revered makers. He sat at the kitchen table with a cup of English tea, took from his backpack a roll of soft cloth and carefully unrolled it. In front of him were delights never seen outside the walls of a museum. The beads, he knew, were extremely rare. They would have a value far above anything he'd seen for a long time, and this evening he would pass them on to Lorenzo Pagano for a profit that would remove the need to work so hard for the rest of the year.

Signor Pagano, as he liked to be addressed even by his close business friends, was someone Steven could happily live without were it not for his unrivalled contacts throughout Italy and the world. Good contacts always meant good business, and Pagano's circle was in a different league, so anything special would always go to him.

He drank his tea with the treasure unrolled in front of him, and was too excited to eat. Pagano would come at seven with his knowledge and his airs and give his most excellent opinion on the beads, and which Steven already knew would be presented so as not to excite the seller too much, and lead to an inflated asking price. No, the beads would be good, very good, *but if you look closely you see these minute flaws, just here... and here?* There were no flaws, but this was part of the game, and Steven was used to it.

At seven o'clock Signor Pagano rang the bell. He was not known for his punctuality, but he would not be late this evening. They sat at that same table, the beads laid out on the cloth as Pagano's eyes ranged over them, betraying nothing. They were each picked up, examined closely, then reverently put back down.

"You have provenance," he said at last, without looking up.

Proof of origin was placed in front of him, and a few old documents. Pagano pored over them in silence then said, "There are thirty-two beads listed here."

"Yes. He's lost the rest, or they were sold, many years ago. He has no idea where they are."

The documents were laid aside. "What do you expect me to pay you for these?"

"five hundred apiece would be fair."

Pagano looked up at him. "Mr Barensson – I don't

think so! Two hundred would be generous, very generous."

So began the necessary game of bargaining, both men more or less aware of where it would end. To Steven's surprise, and the other man's credit, there was no mention of flaws. They agreed on three hundred euros, and shook hands.

Pagano said casually, "A gold cord is mentioned."

"Lost," said Steven, having it coiled in his pocket, and a buyer lined up. Pagano left with the beads and the papers, and Steven rejoiced in being four thousand five hundred euros richer, less expenses. Yes, the day had gone well.

: : :

Just after nine o'clock the next morning, Steven's phone rang. It was Signor Tomasino, the man who'd sold him the fifteen beads.

"Mr Barensson, I have good news. I have found the missing beads, all seventeen of them. I suspected they were here somewhere, and my cousin came and we searched together. So many things in this apartment! Are you still interested?"

A few minutes later Steven was on his way, across the city and a dozen bridges to the university district of

Dorsoduro. Tomasino was waiting and the deal was done, even with the seller's open disappointment at Steven's new appraisal of the beads.

"You see Signor Tomasino, the slight flaws here... almost invisible, but readily seen by an expert. I will have to reduce my offer to you. For these all I can offer is thirty euros apiece."

So Steven improved his profit, and after paying the old man he walked a short distance then sat in a quiet square and called Pagano.

"Signor Pagano, great news! I have the missing seventeen beads. Are you in town?"

But he was on the train to Milan, to see Zennaro, his buyer. He would call again upon his return, so Steven went home with his precious beads and spent the morning in the kind of euphoria he always had after a good deal.

It was the middle of the afternoon when Signor Pagano rang the bell. He was unhappy. His expression was similar to a gargoyle Steven had seen somewhere, a fleeting connection before all hell broke loose.

Pagano pushed past him. *"You sold me fakes!"*

Steven was dazed, as his euphoria was replaced by the worst horror he could imagine.

"Well? What do you say?"

"Signor... I don't know what you mean!" He backed across his tiny kitchen. Pagano stood before him, hands on hips, his anger subsiding slightly into a severe tone Steven had not heard before.

"When you said he'd found the other seventeen I hoped it was not too good to be true. So I went anyway. I took the fifteen to Zennaro, and I was embarrassed. Do you hear me? A person in my position, to be embarrassed by dealing with *fakes!* Do you realise what this means to my reputation with him? You give me my money now, or you will pay in another way, I promise you that. And I will accept a thousand for my expenses."

He took a cloth roll from his pocket and threw it across the kitchen, sending beads everywhere. He then took out the documents, tore them in half and threw them to the floor.

Steven paid him quickly, and without protest.

As the money was counted out Pagano said, "Who is this man?"

"Someone I know."

"*Who?*"

"A man called Tomasino, in Dorsoduro."

"You will visit him, for me. You will tell him what he has done, and you will be very careful from now on. I do not deal with fakes, do you understand?"

Steven understood, and Pagano left with his money.

: : :

Phillip Barensson sat in St Mark's Square at a table outside Caffé Florian, sipping his third coffee and hoping to be allowed to stay. It was just before five, around the time he'd seen the man with the bag yesterday afternoon. In the time since seeing him his imagination had worked an ordinary event into an entire scenario, a play worthy of someone's attention, surely. He looked across the square, barely glancing at his coffee for fear of missing *The Man With The Red Bag*, which was what the mystery person had become.

Then, quite suddenly, he was there. It was him, but this time going the other way, and there was no red bag but as he went past there was something vaguely familiar about him, and not just yesterday's familiarity. Too far away for details, but down at this level it was his shape or the way he moved perhaps, a subconscious recognition. And the almost-blond hair. Then it struck him like a slap to the face: *that's Steven. That's my brother.*

In that moment he was sure, even though he hadn't seen him for three years, since Steven had left England, angry with everyone. He jumped up from his chair, almost upsetting the table, and walked quickly after him. The whimsical scenario was forgotten as Phillip followed him out of the square, right past his own hotel and over Ponte dell'Accademia and into the Dorsoduro district. Now he was sure - it was his build, and the way he walked, a slight rolling of the hips, a so-familiar gait he'd last seen three years ago at a friend's party in England. Unmistakable.

He followed him for almost a mile of twisting narrow streets and half-a-dozen bridges until he stopped and hammered on a door just off Campo San Barnaba. Phillip sat across the square and waited.

Signor Tomasino was surprised as Steven Barensson pushed past him into the front room of the apartment, and slammed the cloth roll down onto the table. He turned back to the old man, and was fierce. "I want my money back. All of it. Those fifteen were fakes. I could have been killed – I had to repay everything."

There was a pause, then Tomasino's reply was casual. "So I have to apologise, and pay you back, which I will, of course. I assume you don't want the other seventeen?"

The casualness infuriated him. *"Give me my money!"*

Tomasino unrolled the cloth and counted thirty-two beads, then opened a wooden box and counted out the money. As he finished, and eleven hundred and ten euros were on the table, Steven said firmly, "And I have expenses. I had to pay him for his trouble. An extra fifteen hundred."

"I will not pay your expenses, Mr Barensson, nor your lost profits, whatever they may be."

Steven was incensed. He hissed through his teeth, *"You need to be very careful, old man!"*

"Yes, I am an old man, and your threats are not helpful. I have repaid you. You have lost nothing with me, so be grateful. I am happy however that you have lost your small reputation for fairness."

A shocked pause. *"What?* You sold me fifteen fakes which almost got me killed and you talk about *fairness!"*

"And you deceived me. You thought those beads were genuine, and you cheated me. So it seems I also deceived *you,* and we are equal now – but in reality less so, because I will allow you to keep the gold cord."

Angry now, Steven moved closer. *"You listen to me...!"*

But Tomasino held up an open hand. "No, *you* listen." As he spoke a figure appeared from the adjoining room, a tall, thick-set man who walked slowly towards them. Tomasino glanced at him and said, "Ciao, Carlo," then looked back to Steven.

"I have many friends in this city, friends who would ruin you if I wished them to. So go now, and leave me alone."

He put out his arm to guide him to the door.

Steven scooped up the money. He was exasperated, his strength draining. He stopped as the door was opened for him.

"You even sold me seventeen more fakes! You call that *fair?"* He looked quickly at Carlo, who watched in silence.

Tomasino said, "The seventeen? Oh, they are not fakes. They are genuine, and I'm surprised you don't want them. Still, I've repaid you, and we are all square. Good afternoon, Mr Barensson."

Phillip watched his brother come back out into Campo San Barnaba, obviously agitated as he turned and said something to an elderly man in the doorway, but too far away for Philip to catch. They had a few words, Steven angry but the old man quite calm and softly-spoken, who then offered his hand, which was ignored. Steven turned from him, lowered his head and started back the way he'd come, away from the square.

Phillip jumped up and followed him, passing close to the doorway where the old man stood looking after Steven. He hesitated, torn between asking what the problem was, and going after his brother. The old man looked at Phillip, shrugged his shoulders and smiled before turning and going back inside. Phillip hurried on, keeping Steven in sight and finally crossing St Mark's Square, then over another bridge and into Calle Dei Albanesi, an alley that led down to the widening waters of San Marco Canal. He stayed back, as Steven unlocked a door and let himself in then inched forward, hoping to see a nameplate that so many doorways seemed to have. As he got closer he saw there was a window next to the door, and as he didn't want to be seen he would walk slowly past and hope to read a name there. But as he approached he became bold and went straight to the door and read the grubby brass name-plate next to it: *Steven Barensson, Calle Dei Albanesi 4248a,* then quickly moved on. It felt as if he'd been lifted out of this life and into another, in that narrow alleyway. He stopped and looked back. He'd found his brother.

Phillip walked on, and out onto the wide, paved *Riva,* busy with tourists, the expanse of water stretching in front of him out to the islands and the Lido far beyond. He needed to think. He'd found his brother, but was unsure of his next move. He walked out to the water's edge and stood with his hands in his pockets, gazing out across the lagoon in the early evening sunshine.

He had three options.

He could go back and knock on that door and hope for a welcome of sorts, or he could go back to the old man and ask about Steven. He could also do nothing, and enjoy the rest of his holiday. There was no doubt the first would be the hardest; they had parted three years before under an almighty cloud and it had taken months for Phillip to get over it. His brother simply walked out of his life, then refused to keep in touch. He had no idea how he would be met now. After running all this through his mind for ten minutes, he decided to go back to the old man, who at least seemed friendly and could be a buffer between them. Some knowledge of

Steven might make it less of a cold call, when the call came, as he was sure it would. Yet his imagination leapt – if it were a mistake he could end up floating in the lagoon, this being Italy after all, home of the Mafia. But he smiled at the thought, and would take the risk with the smiling man, being at least an innocent party. Most of all he needed to know about his brother.

: : :

Phillip sat in his room in the Hotel Violino d'Oro. He had much to think about, after an extraordinary two days. First, seeing this man from the Campanile, then the subliminal urge to find him, and above all the crazy coincidence of them both being there. But it took today to confirm the puzzling feelings he'd had. The affinity, and a sad need to make up with his brother, had never left him. He would visit the old man in the morning, then take his chances with Steven.

If he's stupid enough to fall for it, then he deserves to lose the money. That's what his brother would say, and as Phillip lay in his bed that night he went over the reasons for their falling-out. It was sad, but he could see his brother doing anything, any criminal act, and that was the tragedy. Steven was hard, always wanting success with money but as he grew he became so fixated on it even his friends stood back.

What mattered was always the profit at the end, never the route to it – so *Monopoly* was a game not played – and that's what spoiled him in the end: his eagerness to get one over on anybody.

"Profit is good," Steven once said to him, and Phillip agreed then, but his reputation built up with the years until eventually the fallout was enough to send him away at the age of thirty-eight. He abandoned them all, and their disapproval, for a new life in Italy.

Yet Phillip had often thought, *am I being unreasonable here? When does profit become greed? Only when it harms someone?* He could never properly answer that. Then he thought again about yesterday's coincidence. Is it possible to find someone without realising it? Some sort of magnetism between you and them, that pulls you together?

It was a long night. He remembered everything and everyone, from his indifferent parents to his long-divorced wife, who often sided with his brother. Steven never married, and surely never would, and in a sad moment Phillip wondered if he would ever share anything of value with anyone, while wishing it could be different.

Breakfast alongside the canal was pleasant, as ever, with the shouts and bustling of the gondoliers as a background. As he relaxed he almost looked forward to meeting his brother, to see how he was, to sound him out. All he'd said was that he was going to Italy, and Phillip's calls and messages were ignored so he'd given up trying. But in spite of the portents he still wished for Steven to have changed; it was a worn-thin dream though, unlikely to come true, and in his heart he was truly sad for him.

:::

He left the hotel at eleven, and went straight to Campo San Barnaba. The door was opened by the same old man he'd seen the day before, a courteous man, who welcomed him into his apartment. He didn't expect to meet the brother of Steven Barensson, he said, but it was a pleasure; he introduced himself as Matteo Bozzato.

"I wasn't sure about coming," Phillip said, "but I saw my brother leave here yesterday, very upset... and I wonder what it was about. If it's none of my business, please say so and I'll go."

"Well, it is none of your business, but please stay. Tell me about him."

So they drank coffee in the sunlit room and Phillip told Signor Bozzato all about his brother, and the pain he felt for him. The old man's English was excellent, from several early years working in London, and they talked together easily. He was the owner of *Gallerie San Barnaba*, just across the square, and had been since 1964 - art of all sorts, but mostly antique glassware, and for ten years he'd had a manager in there while he slid into retirement.

Phillip asked the question. "So, can I ask why Steven was so upset with you?"

The old man weighed him up, and after a few moments said, "Ah, well... I repaid him for some harm he did to my business last year, a small and clumsy fraud which he thought was forgotten." He smiled. "I do not forget such things. If someone cheats me, I shall try to make them pay somehow, so I made a plan to do just that. I don't know how familiar you are with our heritage of glassmaking?"

"I'm aware of it, but that's all, I'm afraid."

"Well it goes back to the seventh century, possibly before, and very early glassware can fetch large sums at auction. My plan was simple – to defraud your brother in return for what he did to me. But still I apologise to you."

Phillip said, "My brother is alive and well it seems, and I fear he had it coming to him, whatever it was."

The old man nodded. "I have many skilled friends in this city, and my plan was to present him with some supposedly antique glass beads which he would not be able to resist, then to let him defraud me over their imagined value and for him to pass them on to his usual contact for a vast profit. That contact would then himself pass them on for another great profit. But – as expected – the final buyer was more skilled than the first two, and without much difficulty saw them as fakes."

Phillip was impressed. "That's interesting. So Steven was unhappy."

"Indeed. He had to repay his buyer, and pay his expenses. His buyer failed to sell the beads of course, and was severely embarrassed in front of one of the most important collectors in Italy – Bastian Zennaro, an old friend of mine. I'm afraid I played dumb with your brother, and he was delighted with the deal... a frail old man who has no idea of what he has – perfect fodder for someone like him, sadly. He paid me a tiny fraction of what the real beads would have been worth, and went on his way. He was so happy, so I called him again to say I had more and he came back very quickly, but revised his offer and paid me even less for the rest. But it all went so well!"

Bozzato was smiling broadly at the recollection.

"So he came back?"

"Yesterday afternoon, when you saw him. My cousin Carlo was staying with me as a sort of protection. Your brother threatened me. I repaid him, and did my own bit of threatening, and that's it. Sad to say, but I hope never to see him again."

Phillip was surprised at his own feelings.

"Steven was always a trial, I'm afraid. But the beads must have been convincing."

"They were. Exact copies of early *Millefiori* beads, and supporting documents of course. I have many talented friends here."

They sat in the warmth of the room, with their thoughts, then Bozzato put down his coffee and became serious.

"I believe I did it for an excellent reason. Of course, I am not against profit. All businesses fail without it, and my business is healthy. But your brother was guilty, along with his buyer Lorenzo Pagano, for a mean and inelegant fraud against my manager. I'm sorry to say that people like them are so cocksure, so arrogant, and sometimes they fail because of it. But he is your brother, and I apologise." He paused. "You know, you are so unlike each other."

There was warmth between them. Phillip said, "Will you still pursue him?"

"No point. I frightened him with gentle Carlo, then upset him more as he left by saying the rest of the beads were real, which was the truth. If only he'd known! But the sad fact was that he had no idea of their real value anyway. If he had, he would have gone to someone higher than Pagano."

"So you risked losing them."

"I did, but I couldn't resist and it seems I read him well. He thought he'd had an excellent deal with Pagano."

The window before them looked out over the square to the narrow canal with its gondolas and tourists and the tall white facades beyond, elegant and dazzling in the bright sunshine. The coffee lingered.

Bozzato said, "I would like him to see it as retribution, and I regret not telling him so when he was here. You could of course do that for me, if you wished to."

An interesting thought. "Yes, maybe I will."

"Well if you do, he knows me as Signor *Tomasino*, not Bozzato, and you will shock him again if you tell him that Signor Tomasino has a... *financial connection*, shall we say, to the Galleria." Phillip wondered how Steven would take that. Bozzato went on, "I guessed that he would sell them to his man Pagano, and Pagano would then go to Milan, to Zennaro. That's his usual way. So when Zennaro confirmed that he'd made an appointment to see him, I made sure your brother got the other seventeen after Pagano had left. Those first beads were fakes, of course. Pagano has a high regard of himself, and so has your brother – I'm sorry - but they are just smooth-talking *dealers*." He mocked the word. "Zennaro has no love for that man Pagano. He is not a *Veneziano*, and it was a great pleasure to embarrass him in front of my old friend – but that's our secret – along with my real name, yes?"

"Of course. Are you not afraid Pagano will find you out?"

"Pagano is a coward, and my connections are better than his could ever be. He would be reminded that last year he defrauded me. He will be very angry with your brother, but will not trouble me."

After an hour Phillip left Signor Bozzato, both of them by then having given up apologising – one, about his brother, and the other, over the punishment given. They parted as friends. Bozzato had given him a piece of antique glass, by Antonio Seguso. All Bozzato would say was that it was extremely fine and rare, so Phillip imagined the package he carried away would also be extremely valuable. He went straight to his brother's apartment, wanting to get their necessary meeting over with.

He walked the crowded mile in twelve minutes, stood in front of the brass nameplate, and pressed the bell next to the door. And what a door. *A lick of paint would be nice.* It opened and Phillip was faced with his long-lost brother. There was startled recognition, a less-than-solid handshake, and Steven said, "Well well, my brother from England finds me at last."

"A shock for you Steven, I'm sorry. Took me over-night to get enough courage for this."

"I don't bite Phil," he said, already happy to irritate him by shortening his name. They went into the cramped kitchen. Phillip sat at the table, Steven leaned against the worktop, and the atmosphere was measured, not cordial.

"So how did you find me?"

"I wasn't looking for you, I'm here on holiday. I saw you crossing the Piazza yesterday, with your red bag. Couldn't see you clearly but something reached out to me. An affinity I guess. Can't explain it."

"Well... life is full of coincidences, isn't it."

"Indeed it is." It was already a struggle. "Then I found where you lived."

"You followed me?"

"Yes, I did."

"So you've found me. What's next?"

This was certainly Phillip's brother.

"I've missed you Steven, whether you like it or not. How are you getting on?"

"Well enough. I have friends, and a good business." Then he remembered his brother's - everyone's - objections, from long ago. "And don't worry, I'm not a criminal. I wouldn't last long if I were."

Phillip sat looking at him, and hoped it were true. He studied his brother's face, so familiar... but what defines a criminal? Where are the boundaries?

He said, "Have you been in touch with anybody at home? I've heard nothing of you."

"I left home, if you remember, and everyone was happy with that."

"Not everyone, believe me."

"Oh yes, *everyone*. Nobody approved of me, when all I wanted was a good business. I've got that here. You don't have to be a crook for that."

"I hope you're right."

Steven glared at him. "So have you come here just to annoy me?"

"No, that wasn't my intention at all."

"That wasn't your intention! Wonderful!"

He was losing him, all over again. He felt stupid for even dreaming of him changing, so as his hostile brother leaned against the worktop, arms folded, he took a deep breath and said what he'd been unsure of saying. He would be mad at him, but he was mad at him anyway.

"I went to see Tomasino, by the way."

He had his full attention. *"What?"*

"I went to see him."

"Tomasino?"

"Yes. We had an interesting chat. He's a wealthy man, very knowledgeable."

Steven stood away from the worktop, letting his arms drop to his sides and giving Phillip the look he well remembered – a fierce, intimidating glare.

"Excuse me? How do you know him?"

Another deep breath. "I wanted to be sure you were who I thought you were. I followed you to his place, then followed you here, and your name was on the door. I needed to know, Steven. So I'm saying hello now."

Steven just stared at him. "I can't believe this. So what has that old bastard told you?"

"About the beads."

There was a pause. "And what's this got to do with you?"

"Do you want to know why he cheated you?"

Disbelief turned to anger. Steven raised his voice.

"He's a crook, that's why! And a liar!"

"Not quite. You paid him a fraction of what those beads would have been worth. You thought he was a soft old man, so you conned him."

"What's this got to do with you! He agreed a price!"

"Well of course he did. He wanted to catch you."

"Catch me?"

"Yes - some deal you did last year with your friend Pagano."

A very pregnant pause, then Phillip said, "Tomasino has a financial interest in Galleria San Barnaba."

There was a long moment of realisation. Steven turned, rested his palms on the worktop and faced the window that looked out into the Calle Dei Albanesi. Then he calmed.

"Has he now. That's interesting."

"Yes. And the wrong man to cheat, evidently."

He looked back at Phillip. "You just have no idea, do you, how business works. You're a waste of time. Stay out of it. And stop preaching to me." He came forward, put his hands on the table and leaned towards Phillip.

"So what would you have offered him? Just enough to make your virtuous little profit I suppose! You'll never get anywhere."

"No, I guess not, not in your world."

Steven still glared at him, and the conversation had run its course. Phillip stood up and took his package, and Steven said, pointedly, "Why don't you put it in the red bag. Take it as a memento."

The bag was well used, scuffed and untidy. Phillip took it and saw, in small print, the name *Galleria San Barnaba* along the top edge, discrete enough to impress. He smiled but said nothing as he placed Signor Bozzato's package into it. He rested the bag on the table and said, "So, dear brother, nothing changes."

"Dear brother!" Steven smiled at that. "And what changes would you like, Phil?"

"Not calling me Phil would be one."

"So many then. But hey, you're not so perfect yourself, are you." He kept the smile. "Are you? Perfect?" No response. He sat down heavily at the table. "You know I'm not coming back."

"Yes, I can see that."

"Good. Stay out of my business. I have my life, you have yours. They don't agree, and they never will."

After a moment Phillip put out his hand to his brother, who shook it half-heartedly, still sitting.

"I'll go Steven, and wish you well."

"I won't depend on that."

"But you can. Goodbye."

Then Steven couldn't help himself. The coldness in his voice was shocking. He looked away from Phillip and said, "You're not my brother. You're a waste of time, you really are. Leave me alone."

So Phillip Barensson, at last clear about things, crossed the small kitchen but as he reached the door he turned and said, "By the way, Tomasino wasn't lying.

Those seventeen beads were real. Worth far more than you ever imagined." But then he felt wretched for saying it.

In the silence he let himself out, and walked away from Calle Dei Albanesi with his red bag, striding across St Mark's Square, oblivious to beauty and scattering the pigeons before him. He would dream that night of the man who was still his brother, of when they'd laughed together, and in his heart he knew he would never give up on him.

This story concerns the place now called Lombardy, where the River Ticino crosses the great Padan Plain south of the mountains that define the very top of Italy – and the ancient ruler of that isolated place, two centuries before the Romans swept from the south and gathered it up. In those days it was called Etruria, and the most powerful of the northern rulers was Aranth, who referred to himself as *The Immortal King*. The region he ruled with an iron hand was at the furthest northern reaches of the Etruscan Empire – and was a vast area surrounding its capital of Cassuna, a city split between the luxury of his palace and the mean houses beyond, a city of, in those days, some nine thousand people.

The language of those people, who called themselves *Rasenna,* is long-lost, as is the memory of that king because his cruelties were remembered only until they were forgotten by decree, and wiped from the history of that land. His name became a forbidden thing, erased from books and walls, temples and liturgies and within a generation he was forgotten, and that was the cruellest but overdue punishment for a vain and dissolute villain such as he. Yet I go beyond my story, for I am concerned only with the last seventeen years of his long life, the time between one Favourite, and another.

The First Favourite

Divico, an orphan of the Tigurini tribe of the Helvetii, left his people in the late spring on the eve of his twentieth birthday, and strode into the mountains on the southern rim of his homeland carrying nothing but small food, water, a keen hunting knife and dreams of sunshine and adventure. Two days later he stood overlooking the wide plain that would be his home for the rest of his life. He saw no-one. The land was as empty as the mountains he'd left, yet half a day later as he came in sight of a distant, shimmering city of towers he was accosted by four horsemen. He'd watched them approaching from afar, and as they wheeled in front of him he'd held his head high, unafraid. They took him, roughly tethered behind a horse, to the gates of a palace which opened to the greatest wonders he'd ever seen. They led him through wide streets of white temples and broad apartments, of high pillars and towers and all hung with cloths and banners of purple and gold. Everywhere was beauty and order, the air pure and scented by linden trees lining their way. And the crowds, the beautiful people dressed all in white, coming forward to wonder at the visitor. His hair was long and his beard unkempt, a perfect barbarian from the savage wastes beyond the mountains of the north, and some shrank back from him as he passed by. His hands were still bound, his knife carried by one of the horsemen who had found him. They took him to the inner courtyard of the Palace, and as they crossed from one side to the other the windows and balconies were thronged with the curious and the fearful.

The horsemen had brought him because, above all, Divico was valuable. He was a strikingly handsome, fair-haired young man and they hoped their King would reward them for such a treasure – and if he were not suitable he would simply be killed. But the King was indeed interested in the barbarian.

He ordered him to be bathed and shaved, and dressed in the Etruscan manner, but his hair was to be washed and left as it was, its natural colour a true wonder to the dark-haired Etruscans. His language was of the Celts and unknown to them so servants were sent into the outer city to find someone who could under-stand him, and in a short time they returned with a merchant who had strayed into the land of the Helvetii, been captured, then ransomed three years later. He would talk with him, and so Divico's story was relayed to the King:

"We are called Tigurini, one of the great tribes of the Helvetii. My people would not harm you. We are fierce in defence, and it is honourable to be so. I come to you in peace."

"Why have you come to us?"

"With no intention but for adventure. My people are farmers, my family are dead, and I seek more of the world. I was captured without cause, and brought to you. I offer my friendship." He smiled broadly and bowed to the King, who smiled back and after studying his face carefully, led him away with the merchant to his private chamber where he was questioned into the night.

Aranth had proclaimed himself Immortal King fifteen years before the setting of this story, following the death of his father, and immediately became the tyrant he had been brought up to be. Not immortal, nor the only king, but one of many in Etruria; he ruled a vast region far away from the real power – the great wealth of the landowning kings closer to the settlements that would join to become the city of Rome. At best he should be referred to as My Lord, but distance allowed him his vanity and to call himself *Immortal King* and to insist that others around him do the same. It seems he was tolerated with amusement from afar because of his success in trade, and the abundant funds he provided for the kingdom.

This arrogant egoist was fifty-two years old and in his prime. Physically strong, his rule was absolute and unforgiving and his first deed was to promptly exile his only rival – his more agreeable and much-younger brother – to the city of Caisra, in the far south, then quickly drawing close to him those who would support him and banishing those whose affections were lacking.

Everyone feared losing his favour, which invariably meant death, and yet he, like all Etruscans, bowed willingly to the gods. Nothing of importance was done without consulting the many deities, and if they should prophecy that one would be ill, then one would be ill, or if one were about to lose a battle, that battle would be lost – the will of the gods was final. There was a god for everything and it was a life guided by diviners, who would examine the livers of sheep or watch for all manner of natural signs, such as lightning or flights of birds or the behaviour of water in darkness. They were considered infallible.

The King had three of these diviners, proud sorcerers trained in the art of bizarre observation, and wielding extraordinary power over even the highest in the land, namely the King himself. They were two men older than him and a rare ancient woman of disputed age, and the morning after Divico's arrival he consulted all three with regard to the newcomer. After much ceremony the woman, from her superior position, announced the result: the barbarian would be faithful, he would add prestige to the Court, and the gods saw nothing in the future to cause alarm; thus Divico was unwillingly ensnared into the Court and would soon become the latest Favourite of Aranth, the Immortal King of Etruria.

It was not a simple life at Court. Rules would change at

the whim of the King who would keep everyone guessing, backed up by his Palace Guards and Citizen's Guards beyond, chosen for their indifference to all but him. Savagery and injustice were everywhere and when things seemed at their calmest, they were usually on the verge of some atrocity. "Where is Thresu!" or "Where is Thanusa!" always meant trouble for those people, who should know what the King required of them at all times. So poor Thresu, or Thanusa – perhaps a dancer or a serving girl, would suffer.

And before Divico the three Favourites of the King – boys, youths, androgynous and chosen purely for their beauty, would be available and submissive to his demands. But now Divico, a novelty of handsomeness with his strong, hard features, his ruggedness and his astonishing hair, would take their place. It was widely wondered how long the novelty would last.

He was to learn that a Favourite's loyalty was absolute. Sexual preferences didn't matter to the Etruscans but loyalty to a leader did, and just a whiff of misconduct was enough to end a life or for the miscreant to be cast out – itself almost a death sentence (those expelled often chose to wander the open country beyond Cassuna than face the wrath of the people there, most of whom loathed the King and those who chose to live with him in his Palace of luxuries).

There were sixteen temples within the walled circle of this great Palace, and all facing different parts of the sky, to the sixteen abodes of the gods; but a city cannot support itself with palaces or temples, and beyond the shining white pillars and lofty turrets lay the town proper, the outer city, a mishmash of low buildings, rough and squalid, noisy and forever in movement. It was there that the King's wealth was created: copper was refined, silver worked, olive oil extracted and bottled, and all taken in bulk to the ports to the east and to the south, towards the centre of Etruria.

Cassuna's nine thousand inhabitants were kept in order and submission by the hundreds of Citizen's Guards throughout the city, with divine permission to brutalise and abuse anyone they considered a threat to their Master, or to their own enviable position. The ultimate threat of death was always there, along with expulsion – the casting-out naked from the furthest gate of the city into the wilderness beyond; this great city was a hundred miles and more from the next settlement, the village of Manthva far into the east and lacking even the dubious civilisation of Cassuna. Beatings and executions were common in the city; expulsions happened, but were rare.

The morning after Divico's arrival the King had taken the merchant to a chamber of carved furniture, rich carpets and sumptuous bedding, the walls draped with embroidered tapestries and silks, the ceiling glittering with tiny silver stars. Divico was alone there, and the

King addressed him:

"You will live here, and you will sleep here – or wherever I consider fit for you – but you will live well."

He was to expect visitors, and Divico stood in the middle of the chamber, already realising exactly what that meant, the merchant standing away with his head bowed as he mumbled his translations. Then the King thought it necessary to lightly kiss Divico's lips to get his full understanding, whereupon the young man recoiled but was held close. Moments later the smiling King left them, placing one of the Palace Guards outside the door. The merchant, clearly in terror of the situation, came close and spoke in an undertone:

"I am to live in the next chamber, and teach you our language." Then, almost in a whisper, and gravely, "I fear you are not of his persuasion, you understand me... but he will not be denied, upon pain of your death."

Divico said nothing.

"We are taught from childhood that our bodies are to be shared, but you are for the Immortal King alone. Do not forget that."

The merchant left then and Divico sat with his thoughts. Soon a girl came in with food for him, naked save for a thin golden belt around her hips, her head bowed in subservience. She left in silence.

"I know you have such customs in your country."

The merchant had returned some time later, and

explained the Etruscan way of life, and love, to a subdued Divico who replied, "True, we have warriors like that. They live with other men, and prefer them even over their women. But beyond that, most are faithful to their wives. If I had stayed I would be expected to choose a wife and be faithful to her."

"And would you have done that?"

"Yes."

"So, have I not shocked you?"

"No. As you say, we are as accustomed to this promiscuity as your people are." Then he became thoughtful. "But my response to the King will surely condemn me."

The merchant replied, "No, it will not, unless you repeat it," and the rest of that morning was spent in Divico's chamber where he learnt his first Etruscan words, which the merchant thought should be *Immortal King* and *Yes*, and one day later Divico was indeed the King's latest Favourite, and fully aware that he was not free to leave.

There were women in the Palace, courtesans available to the King and anyone else he offered them to, and officials and their wives, and in their relaxed approach to sex there was much openness and sharing of each other – courtesans with slaves, serving girls with dancers, sometimes men with their wives and the King with everyone, male and female. The only losers were the pretty youths still bound to him, for with the arrival of Divico they were expected to remain faithful, and celibate.

Divico was trapped, himself bound to the King and made to perform whatever he desired, and those desires were fierce. Kept in his chamber, Divico saw no-one save the merchant and the serving girls, and after the first week he realised what his eventual fate would be. A few times a day he would be visited by Aranth or taken to his chamber – moved around like a commodity, a useful thing that he knew would become less useful in time. He had witnessed the death of one of the young Favourites, who in a mad moment had touched one of the serving girls with a hand not controlled, but observed. The guard dragged him to the chamber, where Divico sat with the King and was appalled at the savagery meted out, the violence of the man he was expected to make love to. In the aftermath all the King could say was, "Have you abandoned that smile you first gave me so few days ago?" and Divico was obliged to smile.

He made plans – desperate, dreamy plans. Every day, girls would bring him food. Girls, not women. All younger than himself, and the eldest of them he guessed was sixteen years old, not older. They moved like girls, they looked like girls, dutiful, beautiful. Morning, midday, afternoon, evening. And every day he, like the hapless Favourite, longed to reach out and touch – an accidental touch perhaps, a light caress hardly felt. And with no-one to observe, why not? He knew the girl would not give him away because she would also be punished. Observation was proof. Someone had to see it happen, and his chamber door was always kept closed. So Divico waited for his moment, the small thrill under the shadow of his precarious life, the promise of softness in the midst of severity.

There was a particular girl, one of five who served him on different days, and this girl became special to him. She occupied his thoughts as best she could even when he was pleasuring Aranth, and she became the one he waited for. It happened that one day in his second week she came to attend to the lamps in his room, a process that took minutes more than the simple delivery of food. He watched her as she went from lamp to lamp in silence, in the gloom and then in the light of the flame, her body drifting from shadow to gold.

"What is your name?" His language was poor, but she understood, and knew not to refuse.

"Sethra." She did not look at him, but continued her work. As she left he said, "Thank you, Sethra," but still she dared not look at him, but bowed to him before opening the door.

Every time she came his need for her grew. Her next visit was the same, but the one after that was not: he was in love with this girl, surely. On that visit, after she had attended to the lamps, he called her over to him and held her free hand in his, out in front of her, and after saying Look at me, Sethra three times she raised her eyes to him at such close quarters that all his doubts left him. He just looked at her face, quite overcome, and he did not touch her further, but let her go. She bowed, turned and left him.

Within the hour he was summoned to the King's chamber.

Days passed, and Sethra did not return and when sleep came, he dreamed of her. Another girl tended the lamps, and Divico feared she had been caught out and punished, or worse. He dared not ask anyone. Then on the fifth day she returned, and again he called her to him and held her hand. He took the oil from her and placed it on the floor, then stood up and put his arms around her. She stood like a statue, warm and still, and he thought of all the times she'd surely had to submit to some man or another... and did she find him any different? He held her for a long time, pressing her against himself with his face in her hair, then had to let her go. She went, as submissively as before, bowing to him at the door, and suddenly he knew: *this girl is not afraid, but she has been abused many times. She tolerates me.* What he had in mind would be easy, but without love from her. *She will not feel love for me, not here.* Outside, and in time, maybe she would. He knew that already he had done enough to condemn them both, and after twenty days in this god-ridden place his mind had turned from the excitement as he'd approached the great plain, to the expectation almost of death but with the exhilaration of this solitary girl before that happened.

Two days later she returned, and to his astonishment, instead of tending the lamps she straight away offered herself to him without being asked, and in the warmth and semi-darkness the minutes of exhilaration, of passion, were soon over. Then, back to earth with Sethra in his arms, the future terrified him. He held this girl, whose mind he didn't know at all, for as long as he dared. She looked deeply into his eyes then left him and he stood, looking at the closed door.

It is unbearable.

In the hours that followed he went over the possibilities of escape for them both. He knew the girls went into the city sometimes, and that his position gave him a certain protection, a certain freedom within the Palace. He was no longer kept a prisoner in his chamber, but once outside of it he was watched. *So is it impossible? Is it?* His mind went around and around within the experience of his twenty days. The Palace was familiar to him, the rooms, the passageways, the doorways to freedom, and now those things held different meanings. They gave him hope. The need for escape consumed him, and in some distress he went over the desperate plans he'd made in the days before.

But the day progressed and the plans were to be left where they had grown – in his imagination, because in the afternoon, and shortly before his food would be brought, Divico was taken by two Palace Guards to the King's chamber. Unknown to him, much had happened since Sethra's visit; she had gone with seven other girls for some reason into the outer city, escorted by two Palace Guards, and in the bustle she had slipped away from them, being missed less than a minute later but long enough for her to disappear into the narrow crowded streets. After a frantic search, which involved many Citizen's Guards, she could not be found and the girls were returned to the Palace. It was there that Sethra was betrayed. Two of the girls had seen her coming out of Divico's chamber and had talked with her, quickly sensing something, but she admitted nothing. Their suspicions went with them to the city, and were confirmed when she disappeared and this was told to the guards, and then to the King, whose fury knew no bounds. The guards of the escort were slaughtered in front of everyone: the priests, the women, the court officers. The girls were beaten then sent out with everyone else, and Divico was brought in, along with the merchant. He stood in the open chamber, with the bodies of the escorts lying in the shadows. A guard was each side and the most trusted one close behind him. His thoughts were racing, and his anguish rose until he could think no more. The seconds passed, then the King stood in front of his Favourite and calmly asked,

"So, my barbarian, what do you say?"

The merchant stood to the side and helped him with the language he had not yet mastered, and Divico gave an almost breathless answer: "Immortal King, what should I say? What has happened?"

"Much has happened that you know of, and some you know not of. So you will tell me what you know has happened."

"But what should I know?"

"What you know is that you have abused your loyalty to me. Would you agree?"

There was nothing Divico could say. The King went on, "There was a girl in your chamber this morning, was there not?"

"A girl brings food, and another comes to tend the lamps every day."

"And did that one tend the lamps today?"

"I was there, yes."

"Your lamps are still untended, barbarian. The girl did not spend time with them, but with you."

Any answer would condemn him. The merchant stood motionless, head bowed.

The King moved closer, and the lie came easily: "We have the girl. You will tell us the truth, or she will die. Would you save her? Would you let her be cast out from here, or let her die?"

Divico stared into his Master's face, his heart and mind suddenly full of what he was sure were lies. His time had run out. In despair he gave in to the slight hope that Sethra would be spared.

He said softly, hopelessly, "It is true."

The King glared at him, took a few steps back and glanced at the guard standing behind Divico, who turned his head in the direction of the glance, but too late to see the flash of the sword that took his life. The merchant almost fell backwards with the violence of his friend's death.

"You will find her!" bellowed the King to his guards, as he turned away.

Seventeen years later: The Second Favourite

In the village of Manthva, Thesanthei sat with his elders in the house of the priest. The talk was low, and secretive.

"...and you will do this thing?"

"Yes, I will do it," said Thesanthei.

"How will it be done?"

"Without mistake or hesitation. I will not be persecuted after the act."

The wisest of his elders said, "You are right. There will be no hunger for hunting you down, except to praise you. Will you return to us?"

Thesanthei was certain. "I will see you again – but

now, they are coming."

Moments later the door opened and two men came in, dressed in finery that showed them to be guards of the Royal Palace of Aranth, the so-called Immortal King, at Cassuna, far away to the west.

"Thesanthei is to come with us," one of them said and as the boy feigned reluctance, swords were drawn and he was taken away. The hundred miles were a day and a half of hard riding on horses trained for endurance, and as the city appeared low on the horizon the sun was setting above it, in front of them. He was taken straight to the King.

: : :

Thesanthei, seventeen years old, was a fearless boy. For all his life he had lived in Manthva, knowing only those who had raised him in their customs and language, and watched in awe as his powers of prophecy developed without teaching or effort of any kind. He became a diviner of excellence, a natural, a prodigy. But he was more than that; nothing could be hidden from him, and his ability to look around himself and see the invisible – the energy, the signs of goodness or evil in others, gave him a power unknown in anyone else. He was revered across the northern lands of Etruria, and it was certain that the King would eventually seek him for himself, so it was no surprise to most when he was taken.

Manthva and its four hundred inhabitants felt only the distant tremors of unrest and terror that the King maintained from his palace in the west, and as he grew, Thesanthei learned much of his ways – his cruelties and injustices, his perversions. Then, on his seventeenth birthday, the truth of his own origins – his lost parents – and the certainty of his prophecies came together. He would destroy this Immortal King, end his days on earth and free those who were still suffering under him. It would happen. He had confided to his elders his intent and with their blessing had been taken, as foreseen, across the plain to Cassuna. But now, in the presence of the King he vowed to destroy, his hatred would need to be put to sleep, and his vow would wait until its time came.

In the King's Palace Thesanthei was escorted into a small receiving room, where a man dressed in the Roman fashion of white and purple was talking quietly with the King before bowing to him, then turning and going out. The King leant on an ornate staff, to rest an obviously injured leg; he was an old man of almost seventy years whose robust health had left him, slowly robbing him of movement and response and making those who cared unsure of his self-proclaimed immortality.

Thesanthei approached and faced him, suddenly needing his fearlessness as he found himself in the astonishing presence of the very man who had filled his thoughts for the few months of his eighteenth year, the man who had taken his parents from him.

"Thesanthei – I have heard much of you. You will be happy here."

Happy or not, he knew he would have to stay.

"I will be honoured to serve you, Immortal King."

Then, without delay, he was bold enough to test the tyrant, knowing his own value. "But I would prefer to call you *My Lord*, or *Great Lord*, which is the way the ordinary people refer to you where I come from. They are titles of great esteem, and I hope you will allow me this privilege."

He was given a wry smile. "You are very confident. I trust you will serve me well."

"You must use me to your advantage My Lord."

He studied the boy's face. "So what do the gods tell you of today?"

"That I am to spend ten days here with you."

"Just ten days?"

"I am told it will be enough time, My Lord. There is much I can tell you."

"You will come with me."

They went slowly, the King leaning heavily on his staff and almost dragging his injured leg. In the richest of chambers Thesanthei stood, with a guard each side of him, facing the King – now a poor vision of the Immortal King he imagined himself to be, reclining on sumptuous cushions; the first dark cloud appeared as the boy was stared at in complete silence for the longest ten seconds, during which his resolve was tested. His greatest fear – even while knowing his future – was to become unnerved by the harshness of this man, who finally said, "So you can foretell my future?"

"I can be valuable beyond words, My Lord. I can show you the prophecies of the gods in any situation. I can prepare you for whatever awaits you."

"Go on."

"The injury to your leg was foreseen, and your visitor from Rome."

His reply was short-tempered. "Should that impress me? Those things have already happened. Do better."

Thesanthei bowed his head slowly, and told him of things he had foreseen: "Your injury will be healed in forty days My Lord." A small nod from the King. "Also, the Roman's undertaking will not go as planned."

Silence. The look from the King was a cold glare. It was a thread he did not want to follow, with the guards within earshot.

"You have more... of other things?"

"Your golden chariot will have two of the finest black horses in all of Etruria. Tomorrow at sunset they will come from the northeast, of their own accord."

"Which could be arranged."

"The gods have told me that this will happen. They do not lie."

He was again watched, in silence. "So what is your practice? Are you a reader of entrails?"

"No My Lord. I will not destroy nature, but gather from it – birds, trees, clouds, water, weather. The gods give messages through them all."

"And what do the gods say I should do with you?"

"They say you require me to stay, and will not harm me."

"That much is true."

He sent the guards out. The heavy door closed behind them and he was alone with the boy. His tone was urgent.

"What of the Roman?"

"Alas, his task will be thwarted. The plans you made for your brother's death will not be fulfilled."

This was indeed a grave secret, and in an instant the King was angry. He glared at the boy, then pointed a finger at him. He kept his voice low. "You will tell no-one of this."

"My loyalty is only towards you, My Lord."

"No-one will know!"

Thesanthei bowed his head then looked back at the King. "All that I see is guarded, and for you alone."

"Who betrays me? Is it the Roman?"

"It is."

"And what will happen to him?"

"He will be returned to the Palace, and justice will be served."

The King looked up at the boy standing before him.

"What am I to do with you?"

"My Lord?"

"Do you know everything? Tell me, are there people here that would harm me?"

"As with all great kings, there are those around you who are not satisfied. But you are not in danger from them."

"Give me their names."

Thesanthei already knew the ones who were discontent.

"Several of the lesser priests are unhappy with you for their lack of advancement. You will win them back with small favours. Speak with their elders, My Lord."

The King kept his gaze on him, realising the great value of this boy who was more than a diviner, more than a seer, a source of infinite power for him. There were many questions. *Is my brother really a threat? Will my trade increase? What esteem do I have amongst the other kings?* They were answered in turn as Thesanthei remembered the advice of his elders at Manthva: *Be clever, be flattering. Your words must seduce him. You will need him to be addicted to you. The more he has from you, the more he will need.*

Then the final question, How long am I to live? and the favourable reply, "The gods are encouraging, My Lord. At this time they say you are to have a long life."

After almost an hour the King called for his guards, who helped him painfully to his feet. He would not succumb to being carried, so slowly led Thesanthei through a side door and into a chamber beyond; it was darkened, with few torches around the walls and heavy with the scent of incense. When his eyes became accustomed to the gloom the boy saw with some alarm that it was crowded with women reclining on cushions, some naked, some with scant coverings, but all appearing to him as very beautiful.

"The most perfect women of our race," said the King, with an expansive wave of his arm. "You will have the pick of them." He shouted, "More light in here! Let this man see!"

Torches were brought and Thesanthei was obliged, as though they were cattle, to walk around and inspect each one; he counted nineteen, from young girls to mature women, all beautiful, and all watching him with doleful eyes as he passed by.

"Any of them you wish," said the King.

So he looked at them all, and with some difficulty kept his mind from severe distraction. He knew he would soon have to choose from them, and later that evening one of the priests would take him aside and whisper, *"Choose, but do not make favourites,"* but the boy knew what he had to do.

The Immortal King had indeed been seduced by his

words. Thesanthei's predictions, together with the reputation he'd brought with him, had gained his trust and so in a short time he would become the most-favoured of the King's circle. He had put himself above the pretty boys who were sometimes called to the Royal bed, and would be outside the intimacy they shared. He was held in awe and the King's desires for him - if they were there at all - were reined in, so he would be a Favourite without the duties expected of one.

As it became late, and that first day at Court came to an end, Thesanthei was shown to his chamber. He duly slept that night with Vesia, a woman brought to him from his memory of the nineteen: "the one with sad eyes," he'd said, but when told they all had sad eyes, added, "then she is the one with her hair tied with blue ribbon."

: : :

A few days before, the news had reached the King from a returning merchant, news of prophecies fulfilled, of clairvoyance, of things far beyond mortal abilities.

"There is a boy, Immortal King, who has great powers and has done great things. He would be an asset to your Court."

Accordingly, the King would have him for himself, and sent his most trusted guards to find him, having successfully consulted his three Royal diviners beforehand. He had then sent two of those diviners off to a city in the far south on the pretext of them being needed there, knowing the one that remained would be less troubled by jealousy of the newcomer. The King wanted Thesanthei to himself, without interference, and so the preparation was complete. The prodigy had arrived without ceremony.

The next day, his second, and like all the others that summer, was sublime: the pale blue and vast sky, the light caressing winds and distant heat haze, the dust lifted and blown lazily across the endless plain. He stood before an open window, and in the warm silence the words came to him as he stared out towards the city, repeating his own promise to himself upon his seventeenth birthday, the day the vision of truth had come to him: *my parents must be avenged.*

Life went on around the novelty of the boy Thesanthei. Then at the end of the morning he was called to the King's chamber, where he was offered an exquisite jade knife with belt and sheath, brought to him on a cushion of shimmering red silk.

The King asked him, "Did you know the Chinese value jade above gold?" He did not. The knife was a wondrous thing; the handle was chased bronze inlaid with gold, and the blade the most beautiful pale green jade, pointed and edged to perfection. It was a thing of delicate, ruthless beauty, the belt and sheath of finely decorated leather. The King offered it to Thesanthei, who took it with acceptable reverence.

"This is a gift. It is amongst the finest treasures I have. You will wear it to show your respect for me."

The boy fastened the belt around his waist, sliding the knife into the sheath. He was also given a tunic of the finest cloth, run through with gold and silver thread, and an embroidered, ruffled hat of blue silk. In less than a day he had quietly replaced the King as the focal point of the Palace, looked at by all, his finery marking him out as the favourite of favourites, the chosen one.

The afternoon was spent in the King's chamber, an afternoon of endless questioning and a plausible mix of careful answers, some true, but most designed for flattery. Despite the favourable prophecies the King was frustrated and irritable, unable to make his injured leg comfortable as he lay on cushions and talked with the boy.

As sunset came, with its long shadows and crimson sky to the west, Thesanthei said, "My Lord, your promised horses are approaching. They will raise your spirits."

The guards helped their reluctant Master to his feet, bitterly complaining and awkward with his infirmity, and he followed the boy to a window overlooking the bare plain to the northeast, and there, far out, were two horses, trotting towards them. They came closer, and their coats shone like pure black satin in the low rays of the setting sun. Within a furlong they stopped, facing the Palace. Soon a figure walked out to them and the creatures allowed themselves to be led in to the Palace stables. He turned to the King, and said, "Arranged my Lord, but not by me."

"Then I thank the gods for their generosity," he said, and turned away from him, impressed by the magnificent creatures and their perfect timing... and unable to admit that his spirits *had* been lifted.

On his third day Thesanthei informed the King that a coming earthquake, such as sometimes still happen in Italy, would strike on the great feast day of Tinia, two days hence. The Palace would be spared, he said, but some of the outer city would not. So preparations were made: precious bowls and vases were placed on beds of straw, likewise statues and anything else remotely breakable, and the people waited. When it came, on the prescribed morning, the tremors shook the Palace and destroyed a tenth of the City. And soon after, a source of water, long searched for to the west of the City, was easily found by the boy. This was real and final proof of his skills. Here was a diviner of miracles.

So life went on. Thesanthei spent his days close to the King as visitors came and went, some asking for prophecies, and all in awe of him. All manner of predictions came true, and all adding to the prestige of the Immortal King. Then, as the tenth day came closer, and during their midday meal, the King said to Thesanthei, "I wish you to stay here. Ten days is not enough."

The boy waited, as if in deep consultation with himself, before replying. "It is foretold My Lord, and I know not how to change it. It will happen."

He could feel the frustration.

After some thought the King said, "And where will you go?"

"Back to Manthva My Lord, to my people."

∶∶∶

The vision had not lied to him.

It told him his mother had been hunted for more than a year, and in desperation had left her newborn son with people who promised his safety, then disappeared into the hinterland of the vast Plain of Padan, into the unknown, feared captured or dead. But a year before his vision, he had been told *I saw her long ago,* by someone passing through, and *going north* was the only clue. Thesanthei wondered if she was looking for her lover's – his father's – people, far over those mountains to the north. There were no certain answers from those around him, just concern for the boy while he waited for the truth to be revealed. He would wait a whole year.

Later, when the shock of the vision left him, and using his best skills, all a dismayed Thesanthei could foresee was a faceless woman waiting – but with certainty yearning for him. He saw that she dreamed of returning but feared her child dead, and her own life still in danger. She was settled in her grief.

: : :

In the late morning of his tenth and last day Thesanthei stood at a wide window in the north side of the Palace, looking to the sky, arms outstretched and seemingly oblivious to all around him. He was watching a great flock of birds – a hundred or more – wheeling and crowding together then scattering, before returning to the flock. There were no relevant omens in this cloud, but with the King and a few priests around him it would serve his purpose well. Someone spoke to him but was ignored. He stood as if in a trance until the birds gathered themselves and flew off to the north, then he lowered his arms and turned to see the King close behind him, with a questioning look.

"What did you see? Good things or bad?"

Thesanthei looked at him, feigning reluctance to tell him what he'd seen and his expression was troubled, in the way that an actor's might be.

"Thesanthei! No secrets, not to me! What did you see?"

He lowered his eyes and said, "There is something powerful and bad, My Lord. Powerful and bad... but there is more to learn." He looked up again at him.

"I will watch the sky now that the birds have gone."

"Does this concern me?"

"It is possible, My Lord." He turned away and walked from the room, risking the wrath of the King for leaving without his permission, but all was well. He was followed slowly by him - and the priests - without protest, as he climbed the wide staircase to the first floor, then through painted corridors to the front of the Palace where he stopped in the middle of a small room flooded with light. He went through open doors onto a balcony and stood at the rail. It was noon as he looked out over the gardens at the temples and the faraway city, and soon became aware that the King had arrived and was standing a few steps behind him. The boy was still. He tilted his head to the sky, lifted his hands from the rail and held his arms wide as he looked up at the thin clouds. After several minutes his arms came down and he let his chin fall to his chest. The King came closer.

"Tell me, what do you see!"

Thesanthei turned, but stared past him with faraway unfocused eyes and a vacant expression, keeping the look for several seconds while the King stood, anxious and pathetic, leaning on his staff. Then with perfect timing a crow croaked from a tree in the gardens, and Thesanthei turned back towards the sound. He spoke, still looking out.

"Oh, Great Lord, the signs sadden me. There is sadness everywhere, in the clouds, in the wind, and even the crow is saddened." Thesanthei turned back to him. "A weight of bad news is upon me, and rather I should die than tell it to you."

"What is it! You will tell me!"

"My Lord... oh, My Lord, the gods say that soon the hour of your passing will be here. I could not tell you before of this as the signs for such a time must be certain, and only now am I certain."

The old man became older. He stared at Thesanthei, then away to the distant city, shimmering in the noonday heat. He leant heavier on his staff. The well-timed crow left its perch silently with slow beating wings as it disappeared from view, and the two stood together, one young and one old, one destined to live and one to die.

"When will it be? What will happen?" the King's voice was low and soft, making him sound for all the world like a sensitive man, such was the devastation to his spirit.

"It will be this night, Great Lord, in the very early morning, and you will lie in your bed as the gods take you. You will not be alone. There is much glory ahead."

The old man said nothing, but lowered his head and

shuffled painfully from the room, followed by the dismayed priests.

Within the hour the whole Palace was aware of the prediction of the boy Thesanthei. Aranth, the doomed King, sat in his chamber with his priests and advisers, his women and his guards. There were tears – most for the occasion but some for the man, and he was gratified. Two boys, his Favourites, sat at his feet, one quietly sobbing, the other staring into space and possible oblivion, because it was known in the past for a king to take his Favourites with him to the afterworld, even if they were barely more than children.

There was much to discuss, and to arrange. The royal bedchamber was cleaned and decorated, the lamps prepared, the floor scattered with fragrant lime leaves and the incense burners filled with the rarest oils, all to ease the journey of the King. All worked with purpose, some fearful of what would come after, but most with a secret air of relief, and the remaining diviner – a man of seventy-two years – kept low, unwilling to contribute in any way to such a momentous prophecy; Thesanthei was the chosen one. He would be listened to, and believed.

: : :

In the evening the Palace was hushed. The Immortal King of Etruria went to his bed as the light failed, as numerous priests, officials and many others assembled in the adjoining room. People came and went, the important and the necessary, those who admired him and those who secretly wished him gone, until at last he was prepared and ready to be left to the gods.

Thesanthei had waited to the side, and came forward as the last visitor left. The closed door would be guarded from now on. The room was darkened, the rich hangings of purple, gold and silver filling the shadows.

"Thesanthei, my friend. Do you have more for me?" His Great Lord was calm, an old man on his deathbed, reconciled to his fate.

"Only confirmation, My Lord, of the glory that awaits you."

The lamps flickered in some low draught, and the warmth was oppressive. Thesanthei was gratified to see what the tyrant had become – a weak, sickly man, vainly tucked into his richest bed linen with just his head visible, and the magnificent overblanket, heavy, embroidered with silver thread. There was a thin cap on his head, of red silk. He was pathetic, and vulnerable.

He was thanked for sparing his Favourites, the two boys: "You are gracious My Lord, in your pity and your compassion towards them. They are young, just beginning their lives. I thank you."

His Lord merely nodded slightly, accepting thanks

for the mercy he would not have shown but for the boy's request – out of the fear he had of refusing something so trivial from his diviner, his connection with the gods.

It had been arranged that the women and the priests would come to the bedside late in the evening and stay with their King, to give him solace, but Thesanthei would be gone long before. He planned his move in the full knowledge of the outcome. All visitors were denied except for him – and he would leave the room, unsuspected, through the door which would be closed behind him and guarded. He would say the King was sleeping and had requested solitude, then move through the assembled throng and out into the centre space of the Palace, where he would be observed in deep communion for many minutes, until he felt above suspicion when he would make his roundabout way to the northern gate and step out into the darkness, a free man. As foreseen, he would not be pursued.

But now he stood over the bed looking down at the tyrant. He would wait a while, and make conversation with this man if necessary – but an hour passed almost in silence until Thesanthei judged the time to be right. He began his practised words.

"It is soon time for me to leave you My Lord, but may I talk with you a little more?"

"I do not wish you to leave. You may talk, but only of great things, and of promise."

"Yes, My Lord. You know all that has gone before will be remembered, and cherished forever. Your mortal life will end, the gifts you have given will be returned to you, and the glory that awaits you in the afterlife will have the unmatched brilliance of all the centuries of the existence of this land. You will not be outshone, Great Lord."

He was indifferent, being well used to such lavish praise. "You say my gifts will be returned?"

"The gods say they will be returned in all their abundance, as part of the cycle of life, and death. You will be richer than ever before, in death. Do not be afraid."

"I am not afraid."

"Those whom you honoured with gifts, will be more honoured to return them." He touched the hilt of the jade knife. "Even this will come back to you – the greatest treasure of my life, the greatest gift, but it cannot be kept once you are gone. It will be upon your breast and it will journey with you." He looked down at the old man in the sumptuousness of his bed. "What memories you must have, Great Lord."

He saw the merest glint of a tear in his eye.

"Indeed. I have had a long life."

"And regrets? Do you have any?"

"Only that I cannot live longer. That is denied even

to me."

The air was heavy with incense, and too warm. The lamps were steady now. He had clearly accepted his fate, and with a soft expression, a slight smile, he looked up at Thesanthei. The traits of arrogance, of rage, were dimmed, and he was an old man, as frail and ordinary as any other.

Thesanthei said, "You remember your Favourites, Great Lord? And the gifts you bestowed upon them?"

"Yes. I was indulgent to them all."

"And... were they all faithful to you?"

There was a sudden wariness. After a long pause the King replied, "There were... *disloyalties*. They were all dealt with. All of them."

No. Not all of them. Thesanthei's hatred was fully awakened, and his time had arrived. Keeping his voice smooth, he said, "So you will remember Divico, who came from the north, many years ago. The fair one - you remember him?"

The answer came slowly, and with a sense of foreboding.

"Divico... yes, I remember. The barbarian. Why do you ask after him?"

"He was killed here, in this Palace. And over many months the mother of his child was hunted for. She was Sethra, a beautiful woman, and the child disappeared."

"No, no - the child was found." His brow had furrowed with the memory, as his uneasiness grew.

Indeed, the vision had also told of a poor girl and her infant son, who had been taken by the Palace Guards in desperation, and killed to deceive and placate their master. He would avenge them also. There was a long pause before Thesanthei answered; he placed his right hand on the hilt of his knife, and the movement was noticed.

"The child was not found, and lives, to this day."

In the silence that followed, Aranth the Immortal King of Etruria came to an understanding, as a single memory came out of all the years of his life. His eyes were still fixed on Thesanthei's face, his thoughts racing – *So where has this prophecy come from? Who is this boy? It cannot be so!* Sudden anger flared in him, then calmed, as his world turned upside down. He looked across to the closed door – a shout would bring the guards, but death would come before the door could open. There was no escape for him.

Now Thesanthei's vision was resolved. Here was the man who had killed his father, because of his father's love for another. The tyrant's time had come.

The King looked back at the boy, and at last he said, quietly, and with a slow, accepting nod of his head, "I understand everything." Then, "You have his face. I see it now." He could only stare helplessly, his arms fatally tucked into his bed, at the impostor standing beside him. "What will you do?"

Thesanthei smiled, and leaned over him. His voice was soft. "A simple thing. I will avenge my parents, *Immortal King*."

He took from his belt a small vial, and held it between finger and thumb in the face of the King, at the same time drawing the knife with his right hand. The thin, deadly liquid in the glass tube shone like gold in the light of the lamps. His voice was slow and soft in the heavy air between them.

"You see the choice I give you. So now I ask *you*, what will you do?"

There was a moment's reflection, a few seconds as the old man looked at him with eyes still piercing and cruel before demanding, in a voice cold with hate, "It will be quick, and certain," and thus the Immortal King was reduced to a mortal man. Then the equally cold reply, "You do not deserve it to be quick, but it will be both."

Another moment passed and the tyrant closed his eyes, and, consumed with humiliation, the certainty of death and the realisation that he was beaten, he allowed the vial to be emptied into his mouth. There was a brief convulsion and Thesanthei was ready to stifle any cry with his hand, but there was none. In the silence, Aranth the Immortal King was dead. Then, before the gaze of his half-open, unseeing eyes, the exquisite jade knife was placed on his breast, and Thesanthei's vow was fulfilled.

: : :

The sun rises clear and golden in the azure sky over the great Padal Plain on this first morning of Aranth's death, as those left behind – the women, the priests, the nobles of the Palace, the innocent children and the people of the outer city – prepare for happier times. The dead King's supporters are flushed out, gone, and the brother of Aranth is being summoned by those who had kept him in their hopes and their hearts and will welcome him, and trust him to the Palace Guards who would now be devoted to him alone. Meanwhile Thesanthei, the son of Sethra and Divico of the Tigurini, approaches the mountains to the north, seeking his ancestral home and the unknown face of his mother; he strides with certainty and the rising sun, guarding that same smile of his father's that had captivated – and ultimately destroyed – Aranth, the Immortal King of Etruria.

It seems to me that if the sky isn't a shade of blue, then it's one of the many shades of grey. In the past week I've become quite fond of grey; it doesn't depress me any more, as it sometimes used to. I should explain.

In our family, upsets arrive in groups of three. We've come to expect it. No twos without threes – that's our motto. So my younger brother's had detention at school – to everyone's shame – and I've broken up with my girlfriend Vanessa, to everyone's dismay, especially mine. That's two. A third upset was impending, and we did some serious fretting - but then, to our immense relief, number three came along last Sunday. It didn't happen to us directly, not quite, but we grasped it all the same, we were so keen to get it over with.

It was my Uncle Hubert who gave us number three by dying in a rather interesting way, which was quite unlike him. What I mean is, he managed to be helpful to us, and interesting, both at the same time. I suppose I should speak well of the dead, but nothing really comes to mind... he wasn't what you'd call a nice person. I remember his advice to me over Vanessa – "Leave them all alone", he said. Thanks Hubert.

Anyway, to get back to this *grey* thing. Hubert's wife, Flora, was – still is of course – my father's sister. That's not important, but there it is. And she's an artist, so works with colours, which is where the grey comes in;

but first, a bit of background.

All those years ago she fell for Hubert, simple as that. Thirty-one years old, wrapped up in her work, and wondering about companionship. She was 'flippant with her life', as she later put it... could have done better, should have thought longer, whatever. She was a rising star in the art world, into literature and music and deep thought, and so... she married Hubert.

"Oh, but he was handsome," she said to me once, "and he understood me. We liked the same things then."

Well maybe so.

Hubert sold insurance. He was eight years older than Flora, and already his working life was littered with the debris of wasted visits and feet in countless doors - he was a great believer in pushing, was Hubert. He regularly changed employers, a process he called 'giving someone else a chance', as if none of these firms were aware of his genius. Flora went on quietly selling her paintings, and brought in more money in a couple of months than Hubert did in a year of banging on doors, so he gave up work. He just stopped. Five years into the marriage, and he gave up. At least that's how it looked to everyone else... but Hubert wasn't stupid. He would be Flora's agent. He would look after his wife's interests – which coincidentally were also his. She didn't need this, of course, but he somehow convinced her she did.

They lived at Bexhill then, in a small *unworthy* house, as Hubert said, although it was mostly his ineptitude that had kept them there. Anyway, twelve years after his career change, Hubert's father died and left something much grander to his only son, who wasted no time in moving in. The garden delighted Flora but infuriated Hubert, with its vague borders and riotous planting; he wanted order, he wanted tidiness, he wanted a gardener. So someone came, who also had an interest in classic cars – and it was this young man who was to introduce Hubert to what was to become his greatest love, his passion, and ultimately his nemesis. Because, you see, after many years of being out of love with his wife, Hubert fell in love with a car.

It's true, he really did.

That's an age ago now, and Flora was soon quite sick of the presence in the garage. It hadn't moved in all those years, and been fussed over ad nauseam. Not every-one has an E-Type Jaguar in their garage, said Hubert; no, such a shame we have one in ours, said Flora.

Poor Hubert. It was me who found him last Sunday afternoon. Me, summoned by the unanswered tele-phone and a growing feeling of something – but more of that later. The week before (a troubling week for us, if you remember) I'd met Flora in the woods as I sometimes did when we walked our dogs. It was damp and misty. She said to me, "How would you describe this morning, Alex?" That's me, by the way – never Alexis. Too proper.

"Um... misty, overcast, damp. Not cold though."

"And what colour would you say this morning is?"

I looked around. "Well, grey, mostly."

"Exactly!" she said. "And would you say it's a bad morning?"

"No, I don't really mind this weather."

"HAH!" she said, and made me jump. I looked sideways at her and asked if she was all right. "My husband complains too much about the weather. Wish he'd find somewhere else to live."

She told me Hubert had promised to take Jasper – he's their dog – that morning, but when he got up and looked outside he changed his mind.

"He went on and on about the bloody depressing weather, so I said never mind, I'll take him. He was happy with that."

I mumbled, "I'm sorry..."

"He's always saying how grey everything is – what's wrong with grey?"

"Well," I said, "it's very British to complain about the weather."

"But why? – what's wrong with this?" – she waved her arms, to include everything, and went on, "I said to him, if you hate grey so much, why did you have that damned car painted grey? And do you know what he said? He said Flora, my Jaguar is *silver* grey!"

This was a strange preoccupation with grey. After a bit of her usual deep thought, she said, "Grey is a wonderful colour, you know. It's fog and clouds, mist and half-light, totally natural. But what do people say? They say old and grey, *cold* and grey. I'll bet Roget put it in with dreary and depressing. We have grey areas and grey hairs, even grey squirrels are pests. It's all negative, Alex."

I feared she was losing her grip. After a pause, I said, "Why not have a break from old Hubert?"

She said, "Well, I tell you, if he says to me just once more how grey and miserable the weather is, I'll leave him."

I was shocked, but I believed her. This *grey* thing sounded like the culmination of years of small annoyances with Hubert. She'd settled on a reason for leaving, and that's what she did, early on that special Sunday morning. It was Monday afternoon before she turned her phone back on and we were able to tell her about Hubert. She was genuinely upset. She came back that evening to the big empty house, then answered questions from a less-than-enthusiastic police officer. Flora felt she was guilty of something, but wasn't sure what, and after a few indifferent questions he left her to herself.

When I went to see her next day she told me everything she'd done. No secrets, she said. Apparently she'd meant what she'd said to me in the woods, and was soon making plans to go. She said when she got home that day she found Hubert yet again polishing his car, and mused on the prospect of leaving – delicious on the one hand, worrying on the other. Do people really leave home at sixty-two? What do they leave behind? Thirty-one years – half her lifetime – and everything else. He could keep it all though, and she would start again, in a different place. She longed for the relief of being alone, could weep for it.

She'd been well into this reverie when Hubert came in and said, "You should see her, Flora – a lot of work, but she's *beautiful*. You can really see your face in her!" And that was it. That gave her the idea. She said she actually felt sorry for him then, because he knew nothing about what she really wanted. He would miss her. She felt guilty, then defiant – he can look after himself, he's capable. It was that same evening that she finally made up her mind. They'd been sharing the TV and the weatherman had just said, "Quite a grey start for most of us, I'm afraid."

Hubert said, "Bugger, I was hoping to go for a walk first thing," and as he pressed the button on the remote and picked up his Saturday paper, Flora began planning her Sunday. She told me how easy it was from then on, how tough dilemmas can seem trivial once decided. By first light, she was asleep on a train.

When I arrived later that morning, I wasn't quite prepared for the bizarre tableau in Hubert's garage. He was sprawled across the bonnet of his beloved Jaguar, quite dead, and he slid quietly to the floor when I touched him. I was suitably shocked. Poor Hubert.

I went back up to what had become my aunt's house and cuddled Jasper, who was happily unaware of the day's tragedy and wagged his tail. I let him out into the garden, called for an ambulance, then went back to the garage, to the dead uncle and the shiny car.

Of course, Flora had taken an artist's revenge on her hapless husband. I stared at the bonnet of the Jaguar, at the portrait of the wife that Hubert had lost in life and embraced in death, and which I reverently removed without too much difficulty while awaiting the ambulance. *No harm done, Hubert – she's as lovely as ever.*

Flora had really thought he'd get over it.

As we sat together she told me how she'd left a note for him at the top of the stairs, and she wondered how he'd feel to wake up alone in the house. She saw him flopping down in the old leather chair, not believing what he was reading. Well, I think perhaps he didn't flop at all, but raced out in his dressing gown to his doom, his galloping heart barely keeping up. She handed me the note. It was in her best handwriting, quite large for the sake of his old eyes, and I imagined it being written so painfully and joyfully the night before she left. It said:

"Dearest Hubert, on this most beautiful of grey mornings, I am leaving you. As we've been apart for so long, it seems reasonable to look for happiness else-where while I have a few years left. I will be in touch.

I sincerely hope that you will sometime see the beauty of greyness, as I have. Or at least accept that skies need not be blue to be beautiful.

Your wife, Flora."

There was a PS:

"If you were wrong about most other things Hubert, you were right about your car. I saw my face in it too, and so will you if you care to look. Flora. PPS. You will take Jasper, won't you."

Of course, Hubert *did* care to look, and what he saw was too much for him. Flora will recover, I think.

We talked for some time about the past and the future. I could see her life as it must have been, through all those years with a detached, indifferent husband – trapped, with dreams of leaving – then as I handed the note back to her and got up to go she said something I still haven't recovered from. She said, "Alex, if you promise me you'll paint that car red, you can have it."

I promised her I would.

THANK YOU

To my wife Evi
for her patience, and her support

To Gunnar Ridderström
For permission to use the cover photograph
(the inspiration for The Red Bag)
www.unsplash.com

: : :

Also by Gordon Williams

THE GENTLE RIVER
A Novel

UPRIVER
Peter Matthew Bennett's History
A companion volume to
The Gentle River
Providing an in-depth background
to the historical characters and
events of the Novel

Visit: gordonwilliams.uk